engaging the office enemy

a sweet romantic comedy

kristin canary

To every person who had to grow up too fast.
You are seen.
You are known.
You are loved.

one

· · ·

IF I HAD a choice between poking my own eye out with a fork and staying in this meeting, well, pass the cutlery, please.

Alas, I do not have a choice. So like a good little employee, I sit here and take the garbage that Adolf Jones—the CEO of the one-man company that is Jonesing for Coffee—spews in my direction.

Who names their kid Adolf anyway? I almost feel sorry enough for the man to forgive him for his rude treatment of me, but his snarled lip and meaty finger pointed my way are enough to snuff that small flicker of sympathy.

Leaning back in my office chair, I tug the end of my long purple braid around to my lap while Adolf rails on about the many ways in which I have failed him as a graphic designer and brand manager (the latter of which I never wanted to be anyway). The fifty-some-thing's got a super bushy Fu Manchu mustache draped over his lip like a limp fuzzy snake, and he strokes and rolls it like it's a weapon he's sharpening for later use. His rotund stomach is about to burst the buttons on his crisp khaki-colored business suit as he inhales for another volley. I find myself hoping it happens—something, anything, to break up this little hate fest.

But it doesn't, and he keeps on going. Looks like it's up to me to draw this meeting to a close. What's new? "Mr. Jones, I'm so sorry you feel that I haven't provided you with the results you've needed," I interject in the most neutral—and bored—tone I can manage.

Could I have added in a little more charm? More simpering? Made myself "less than" just to give someone else an inflated sense of self-importance? Probably, and that would make my boss, Nate Birmingham, super happy. But you know what? I refuse to suck up to people, especially ones who don't deserve it. I speak the truth and nothing but the truth—though maybe not all the truth. And yeah, maybe it gets me into trouble sometimes.

Maybe it's also the reason I only have a few friends, a close-knit group I've been lucky enough to call mine even though it makes me slightly terrified that one day they'll leave me too. A few already have.

And yes, I realize that getting married and having babies isn't really *leaving* me (I feel eye-rollingly dramatic even thinking it), but the effect is the same. Once my roommates Lauren and Shelby get married next year, I'm going to be Alexis Matkin, *that one crazy cat lady over on Sandy Street.*

Just need the cat and I'll be set.

"I suppose I shouldn't be surprised." Mr. Jones leans forward, and one of the buttons looks close to coming unthreaded. *Come on, baby. Pop!* "You take little care with your own appearance. I don't know why I would think you'd take care with my brand."

Whoa, now. I literally bite my tongue from responding in kind, because I don't stoop to personal insults. People have their own styles—I'm cool with that. I just wish he hadn't brought mine into it. No, I don't wear the adorable skirts and blouses my friend Shelby-the-kindergarten-teacher does, or the gym-chic clothes Lauren wears, or the hot-mama dresses Kayla does, or Evie's librarian-esque sweaters. But I happen to like the jeans and vintage Thor T-shirt I'm currently rocking along with a pair of Birkenstocks (yes, it's October, but sandals are a year-round affair in California). They're comfortable and every day is casual Friday around here, after all. Even Thursdays, like today.

Don't get me wrong. I actually appreciate Mr. Jones's authenticity in this moment. At least he isn't pretending like he's satisfied with my work or beating around the bush. He's being straightforward. But he's also being super rude, and ain't nobody got time for that.

With an abrupt push away from the desk, I stand. "Sorry, I have another meeting." And I do—it's called lunch with me, myself, and I.

His mouth stops moving, and the last syllable teeters on the edge of his lips. "Yes, well." Lumbering to his feet, he looks around my office and blinks. "It's very hard to focus in here, isn't it, Ms. Matkin?"

"I've told you. It's Alexis." If I could scrub all

familial association with my father, I would. But changing my last name would be scrubbing my association with Kennedy too, and that's never happening. Still. Formality is not my thing. "And I happen to focus quite well in here."

The ninety square feet of space I've been allotted at Birmingham & Co. Media—a small marketing firm in San Diego—is my sanctuary from the boring grays and cool blues of the rest of the office. Every time I see the vibrant green walls with abstract yellow and pink artwork, it energizes me, fuels my creativity. The effect is helped along by the large window to my right that boasts a view of the park down below, verdant and lush and not soul-killing in the least.

Staring out that window—imagining myself there, swinging like a child, hair blowing freely in the wind— is how I survive the monotonous parts of my job.

And the times where I'm being yelled at too, which seem to be occurring more and more frequently, all because my boss keeps handing over the good accounts to his nephew, the obnoxiously charming—and completely fake—Dax Nyhart, leaving me with the left- over scraps.

Mr. Jones clears his throat again, a sound that's a mix between a frog croaking and a heavy truck driving over gravel. "I do hope I can expect better results in the future. My company's products are of utmost quality and deserve to be recognized as the exciting commodity they are."

I cough, managing to suppress a comment about how coffee filters are the least exciting product known to man (especially since I can't stand the disgusting black brew so many people call the elixir of life). See? My boss's lecture on being nice to the clients has had some effect, whatever he may think.

"As always, I'll do my best." Without another word, I usher Mr. Jones out of my office and begin the short walk toward the clear front door. The hallway is lined with motivational posters, and just like every time I pass, I edit them in my brain. (For example, the one that says "If you never try, you'll never know" gets "how terrible you are" added to the end. Why must we pretend that everyone who tries something will be amazing at it?)

It doesn't take long to reach the main office, where there are a cluster of cubicles and about four salesmen whose names I can't distinguish because, despite their varying job titles, they're essentially carbon copies of one another. Same designer hairstyles. Same over-muscled chests they clearly spend hours in the gym achieving. Same crass jokes. Reminds me of Dr. Strange cloning himself in one of my favorite movies, *Avengers: Infinity Wars*—except instead of fighting the evil dude Thanos, they're battling good things like individuality and authenticity.

Between them, the receptionist (Gina), our boss (Nate), tech guru (Penelope), and the other two designers (Dax and Rupert), it's a small office, with HR and accounting being farmed out to another company. There are exactly zero people here whose company I enjoy, unless you count Juan, the janitor who has been known to share his menudo with me on the nights I work past midnight (which has grown more often as of late).

As Adolf shuffles out the door, Gina waves a friendly goodbye to him from behind her plain black desk, then looks at me sideways and writes something in her notebook. It couldn't be more obvious that the forty-something mom of three doesn't like me and believes it her sole mission to report on the misdeeds of everyone in the office. With her high tight bun and prim black suit jacket, she's the exact opposite of my ever-changing hair colors and more casual style. She's only got about a decade on me, but acts like her maturity and wisdom are divine gifts to this office.

"Gina." I nod at her with I-know-what-you're-doing eyes.

Her lips draw into a straight line. "Alexis."

My stomach gurgles and I press a fist against it. Time to lock myself in my office and count down the minutes until six p.m. At least all of my client meetings are done for the day and I can spend the afternoon creating, lose myself for a little bit. I can also take a few minutes to text Kennedy back about her latest boyfriend crisis. Maybe I can convince her to finally leave the worthless guy she's with and move down here from San Francisco. After all, within the next year, there will be plenty of room in la Casa de Alexis.

The as-yet-nonexistent cat will only take up a tiny bit of space, I imagine. Ooo, unless I decide to go for more than one. That would really seal the cat-lady reputation.

Heading to the break room, I grab my lunch out of the fridge and bring it back to my office. My bright blue tumbler is empty, so I trudge back past the Drs. Strange and to the other side of Gina's desk, where the water cooler sits. Tipping my cup under the spout, I turn on the spigot and inhale a breath as a stream of water flows into my cup.

Maybe it's the waxy plants in the corner, the white walls, the air that's always tinged with a smell that's strangely reminiscent of the powdered orange Tang they served at my boarding school in place of real orange juice, but something about this place has always made me feel a little bit caged in. Claustrophobic.

I studied graphic design in college and really do love it. What I don't love is creating art for other people, especially since working here requires me to wear the hats of both designer and marketing guru-slash-brand manager. So are there days I dream about leaving Birmingham & Co., finding a job that's less about marketing and more about the art? Or at the very least, something that doesn't bear the burden of someone's entire brand?

Sure. But the idea of going out on my own, the instability of it all … well, remember what I said about preferring to poke my eye out? There's not really a choice in this either.

Because this job pays the bills, allowing me to be independent—and that's the most important thing. In fact, I'm within reach of finally paying off the mortgage on the partially-owned house my aunt left me nine years ago when she decided to move to Europe on a whim. If only I could get rid of a certain someone who keeps taking all the good clients because he's related to the boss—

"Thank you for your time today, Ms. Longenecker. It's been an absolute pleasure." A voice floats down the hallway, growing louder by the second.

Speak of the devil.

The tall, smug, broad-shouldered devil with a capital D.

Dax Nyhart comes strolling down the hallway with our top-billing client, Aretha Longenecker of Longenecker Homes. Besides being a very genteel sort of person, and genuine to boot, her company sells inspired, recycled products for the home that are legit doing a ton to save the environment. Hers is the mecca of accounts, and who do you think landed it without so much as an audition?

If you guessed the infuriating nephew of the boss, you'd be correct.

"The pleasure is all mine, Dax." Aretha extends her sleek brown hand and shakes my mortal enemy's, her face all serenity and smiles. She's a tiny thing, but that doesn't fool anyone around here. The woman is a brilliant powerhouse, and you wouldn't find *her* yelling at someone she's hired or insulting their clothing as petty revenge for lackluster results her own product was responsible for.

There are three of us who manage accounts—Dax, me, and Rupert, who is nearing retirement and couldn't care less about what clients he gets so long as he can do the least amount of work possible—and who do you think is the one getting all the best clients?

Not me, that's for sure, even though my work is definitely superior. Not to toot my own horn, but I give credit where it's due.

And it's NOT due to Dax.

Just because he's objectively handsome—with his long torso, tan skin, brown hair that's as carefully controlled as his temper, and that crooked smile he throws around like candy—doesn't mean he's talented at anything other than schmoozing.

Water hits my bare toes and I yelp when I realize my tumbler is overflowing. Cursing under my breath, I stop the spigot, drink a bit of excess from the top of the cup, slip the lid back on, and dry my fingers on my jeans.

While I'm cleaning myself up, the front door opens and Aretha's heels on the tile floor punctuate her exit. I watch her clip down the hallway and press the elevator button. Too bad I can't join her, but I've got about three and a half more hours until freedom will be mine.

Temporary freedom, until tomorrow arrives—but I'll take what I can get. Besides, tonight should be fun. I get to hang out with my friends.

"Man, I love working with Aretha." Dax's grating voice materializes beside me, and his snickerdoodles-right-out-of-the-oven scent breezes under my nose. "So intelligent. So kind." He pauses. "So *not* named after ruthless dictators."

I tilt my gaze upward and narrow it into a glare despite the way his arresting, amused eyes lock onto mine. His irises are a mixture of green and gold that I can't help but find fascinating—purely from an artistic point of view, of course. "I don't know what you mean."

My tone is forcefully even. "Adolf is amazing. He and I are best buds."

"I completely believe it." He grins at me in that lazy way of his. "You probably won him over with your cheery personality." Dax grabs a Hershey's kiss from the bowl on Gina's desk. As he unwraps the foil packaging, he doesn't seem to notice that our very married receptionist watches him with the end of her pen in her mouth, clicking it against her teeth, a far-away look in her eye.

Seriously, why is every female so enamored with this guy? Don't they know he's engaged, anyway? I met his fiancée a few months ago at my friend Shelby's performance of *Cinderella*. A real winner, she was—one of those bone-thin women who never thinks she's skinny enough, a perfect duplicate of all the girls I encountered at the Connecticut boarding school my mom enrolled me in after my father died and his big secret came out.

Moving to California after graduation five years later to be closer to my half-sister was the best decision I ever made, even if it led me to be in the same office as the obnoxious man in front of me.

I puff out my chest just a little. "Talent should matter more than personality. And there's nothing wrong with mine."

Gina snorts and I toss her a death glare.

"Never said there was, Rainbow Brite."

Gritting my teeth against the ridiculous nickname Dax gave me on his second week of working here, I arch my eyebrows. "We can't all be pompous suck-ups, now can we?"

He leans in close, and my body rebels against my better judgment as a shiver works its way up my spine. "No, but I can teach you some tricks to succeed, if you'd like."

He thinks his nearness is intimidating, but it's not. I step closer, so he'll know *I know* what he's trying to pull. "How's that, when all you really need to do well at this company is some good old-fashioned nepotism?"

And here's how I know he's a complete faker, because that comment would bother any mere mortal, especially a man (because men in general are nothing if not proud creatures who like to go around beating their chests and declaring their own prowess). Yet Dax stands there, looking at me, still smiling and completely nonplussed. "Admit it, RB. I just do my job really, really well."

"Hmm, I don't recall flirting and brownnosing being part of our job description."

"It's called improvising. You should try it."

"One of us has to take this job seriously."

"Some might say too seriously." He tilts his chin. "You work too hard, RB."

Is he for real? "And you don't work hard enough."

Someone clears a throat nearby and I startle, pulling my gaze momentarily from Dax to the bank of eyes in the cubicles across the room. And now the Drs. Strange are flashing identical grins at each other and us, a murmur building between them. I roll my eyes and start moving toward the hallway.

But a hand on my upper arm stops me.

Dax's touch burns into my skin and I shake him off. "What?"

He's close, again, and I lick my teeth to keep from noticing the way the purple polo shirt he's wearing pulls taut against his shoulders, makes his eyes pop. "Admit it, RB. I make this job more fun."

Huffing out a caustic laugh, I shake my head. "That's exactly the type of thing I'd expect you to say. You really don't have a clue, do you?"

"A clue about how much you'd miss me if we didn't work together anymore?"

What a strange thing to say, but then again, I'm used to the most unusual drivel coming from his mouth.

There's only one way to deal with prideful jerks like him. Throw them off their game. So I curve my lips into a sweet smile and look at him with what I hope present as wide, adoring eyes. "Dax."

For a moment, something flickers in his eyes—like he doesn't quite know what to make of me, like the mask he always keeps so securely in place slips just a little. Well, good. Fakers are the worst and he's as fake as they come.

"Yeah?"

"I would miss you"—my words are pure honey in the air—"about as much as Captain America misses Red Skull."

"Huh?"

Oh my goodness. Does this man seriously not know his Marvel trivia? "I can't even with you." Once again, I start toward the hallway.

"Wait, RB." A pause. "Alexis—"

I turn to tell him to leave me alone, but he's closer than I think and I ram into his solid chest, water sloshing out the straw hole in my lid onto both of our shirts. He throws a hand on my hip to steady me.

And I feel that grip all the way to my toes, its zap as sudden and unwanted as lightning. Our gazes collide and I'm close enough to see the slight dusting of stubble on his jaw. He opens his mouth to speak—

"Yo, Nyhart!"

One of the Drs. Strange shouts Dax's name and he blinks, then takes a step back from me. He glances up just in time to see a football sailing through the air. One-handed and calm, he reaches up and grabs it—to a wild round of cheers—then hauls back and returns it to the dude. He shoots the guy a thumbs-up and the mask is fully intact once more.

Clearly, it's not just women who are obsessed with Dax Nyhart. Everyone else falls so easily for his lies and manipulation, believing he's really a good guy who is genuinely happy all the time.

But no one is happy all the time. Everyone is hiding something. And I don't trust the ones who pretend they aren't. I've done that before—twice. First with my dad. Then with Corbin. And twice, it's come back to bite me.

I refuse to be the fool who falls for it a third time.

So while Dax is preoccupied, I retreat to my office, lock the door, and eat my lunch alone.

Just the way I like it.

I told myself I'd leave on time today. I have to—Shelby's counting on me to be at the bridal shop at seven p.m. sharp.

But just as the sky is turning a gorgeous pink outside and I'm about to pack up, my boss breezes into my office. "Alexis, we need to talk." Nate takes a seat across from me and twiddles his thumbs, shifting in his chair. "I heard about your meeting with Adolf today."

My first thought is that Dax told him, but he doesn't know the details of it unless he could hear Adolf's yelling from his office next door—a distinct possibility, given how thin the walls are around here. But what would be his motivation?

Wait. He said something about us possibly not working together anymore. Is Dax trying to get me fired? Even though I loathe this job, it's the only thing allowing me to pay off my bills. Unlike my sister, I wanted nothing to do with my dad's life insurance money and donated every cent I got upon my eighteenth birthday to a program that provides art scholarships to underserved youth. At least some good can come from the man who betrayed everything he claimed to believe in.

My stomach bottoms out and I scoot my chair closer to my desk, press my toes into the soft leather of my shoes. Nate's a nice enough guy. Though he must be in his early fifties, he's fit and his full head of hair is only streaked with gray, not consumed by it. He's never spoken harshly to me, even if he's been firm. Surely he can be reasoned with. "Nate—"

"Look." He taps a finger on the edge of the desk, the one monochromatic thing in this office that I can't paint over and have to live with in its boring whiteness. "I know Adolf Jones is an arrogant son of a gun, but he's also a client. And he's not the only one who has complained."

So Adolf himself must have called Nate directly. Dax is off the hook, for this, anyway.

I grunt. "He's just upset that his products aren't selling and that's not my fault. No one wants his lame coffee filters. I've tried them." Well, my housemate Shelby tried them for me, since I despise coffee in all its forms. "They leak and smell like curdled milk. Not even the most effective marketing in the world could sell them."

"And yet, that's your job, Alexis."

Ugh, don't remind me. I attempt to sit up straighter despite the heaviness pervading my shoulders. "I'll do better. I promise."

He nods, but waits, his tapping finger increasing in speed. Then, utter stillness. "Your graphic design, the marketing, is only part of the job, you know. We've talked about this before, but you could try being friendlier. Less—"

"Authentic?"

"No, but you don't have to say everything that pops into your head."

"Oh, believe me. I don't." I inhale sharply, heat gathering behind my eyes. But nope. No way in a Black Vortex am I going to cry. I don't do that anymore. Ever. Most things can be resolved in other ways, and those that can't, well. That's life.

But maybe I can reason with my boss. Not that I haven't tried before, but maybe this will be the time that my words click. "Nate, I believe I conducted myself with the utmost decorum today. Truly. Mr. Jones insulted me to my face in a really derogatory way, and I didn't insult him in return. That has to count for something." Deep breath. Here goes nothing. "But, I do feel that you tend to give me the most difficult accounts while Dax—"

"Not this again." Nate massages the back of his neck. "Alexis, I'm not giving these accounts to Dax on a whim. He's proven he can handle the smaller accounts first and has worked his way up."

"And I haven't?"

His mouth sets into a firm line. He doesn't say anything more, but his answer is obvious.

Fine. "What can I do to prove myself, then?" Because I want the bonuses that come with those prestigious accounts. Need to pay down that mortgage before my roommates move out. "I'll do anything it takes."

"Anything?"

Thankfully, I don't have to worry that Nate is going to suggest certain favors be exchanged here. He's obsessed with his kids and wife, a lawyer who works on the third floor of our building and with whom he eats lunch every day. Personally, I wouldn't trust him—or any man—with my heart, but he does seem like a good man.

Still, I'm going to clarify my stance. "Well, nothing illegal. Or disgusting. Or degrading."

"Of course not." His lips twitch. "Although I'm not sure you'll love my suggestion."

"What do you mean?"

There's a bit of a pause while he shifts, crossing one leg over his knee. "Okay, you want to prove you can handle some of the bigger clients? Work with Dax on a few of his accounts. He can show you how he does things. Take notes. You can help each other." A pause. "If he tells me that you've done a good job, worked well together, then I'll assign some of those clients to you and give you first crack at the next few new clients."

Whoa. I sit back against my chair, hard. What an opportunity.

But at what cost? My sanity? Dignity? Because there's something just a little bit sour about having to "train" with Dax when I've been doing this job three years longer. "I …" Oh man, I want to blast my boss, but I can't. This might just be my shot. Nothing else I've done has worked.

But working closely with Dax?

My jaw tenses as I grind my molars. There's nothing for it. "I appreciate the chance." I cock my head. "But don't you want to run this by Dax first?"

Nate waves his hand in the air. "He's very easygoing about stuff like this."

I can't help the way my spine stiffens at the familiarity with which Nate speaks about his nephew. And of course he does. They're family. It's the whole reason Dax got this job in the first place. But Nate's giving me a chance to use his implicit trust of Dax to my advantage. If I can win over Dax—at least get him to confirm that I'm good at my job, that I can handle more—then I'm one step closer to my goals.

But given our history, that's a big "if."

Seemingly satisfied, Nate stands. "Great. I'll let Dax know and you two can discuss it tomorrow."

He leaves just as swiftly as he came, shouting good-byes to my coworkers down the hall before turning toward Dax's office.

Groaning, I place my head in my hands and blow out a steady breath. But my exhalation comes out rough, streaming between my teeth, stuck in my throat. Because the last thing in the world I want right now is to think about how embarrassing this situation is going to be.

I told Nate I'd do anything, but I will not—I repeat, will NOT—suck up to Dax. In fact, *he's* going to have to prove to *me* that he has something useful to offer.

And I seriously doubt he does.

My phone buzzes from inside my Avengers-themed backpack purse. I dig inside, check my device, and swipe away the notification. I'll have just enough time to swing by Java Awakening and grab Kayla (and a sandwich) before heading to the bridal shop.

An hour later, after fighting terrible traffic and listening to Kayla bemoan the negatives of owning a small business (e.g., no paid maternity leave), I stand on a dais in front of a bank of mirrors showing off my body at every angle. And lemme tell ya—nothing is worse than feeling betrayed.

Because as I gaze at myself in a lavender bridesmaid dress, I can't help but feel like Shelby has completely stabbed my individuality in the back. "It's … nice."

My petite blonde friend approaches from behind and places a hand on my shoulder. "I know you hate pale colors, but look." She picks up my braid. "At least you match."

"And you look hot, you sexy thang, you."

I roll my eyes at Kayla's wolf whistle. In the mirror, I can see her and Evie lounging in comfy chairs behind us, feet kicked out in front of them. Their hands alternate making the journey from a big bag of Doritos stuffed between them to their mouths. My two former roommates are now married and both about seven months pregnant, due only a week or so apart.

Thankfully, Shelby's wedding to Eric is in July—about nine months away—but not-so-thankfully I'm one of the only bridesmaids available to model the dresses Shelby's considering. Her sister, Deb, is at her daughter's soccer tournament in Arizona, our other roommate Lauren is currently in the dressing room trying on another option, and Kayla and Evie wanted to see what the dresses would look like on a body that's "not currently competing for the World's Most Blimp-Like Object" (Kayla's words, not mine).

"Of course I look hot," I say—because she's right, and I'm not afraid to say so. I may have a small chest paired with some wide hips and the same round rear as my mother, but there's no point in not embracing what I was born with. Women in general spend too much time criticizing themselves and not loving the things that make them unique works of art. "That's not the point."

The point is, if there's anything I hate more than fake people, it's dressing up. In fact, other than fancy nights out with my friends and weddings, the most dressed up I get is occasionally adding my favorite yellow blazer to my normal work ensemble.

But I love Shelby—all four of my current and former housemates—and I'd do anything for them. So here I stand in a strapless, A-line dress that hugs my curves and makes me feel exposed in every way.

Yay.

"I wanna look sexy again." Kayla sucks on the tip of an orange-powdered finger and glances at Evie. "Remember when we were sexy?"

"Oh, please. You barely have a tennis ball under there. Me and my ultra-sized basketball, on the other hand ..." Evie laughs and struggles to sit up straighter. Her shoulder-length brown hair is pulled back in a ponytail and she's dressed in a cotton maternity skirt and blouse. "Besides, I wager Josh still finds you plenty sexy, Kay."

"True." A grin curls on Kayla's lips. "The other day, he showed me just how much."

Oh, come on. "We do not need to hear about your sexual pregnancy escapades, thank you very much." I stick my fingers into my ears and sing LA LA LA as loudly as I dare, but I see Kayla's eyebrows wagging and the rest of my friends laughing even if I can't hear them.

They like to tease me for my hatred of PDA, for the ways I call all men pigs, for my negative views on love. But I have to speak as I find. And what I've found is that the male species in general, with very few exceptions (basically, Connor, Josh, Topher, and Eric), is fickle when it comes to love. They don't stick around. They aren't there when it matters.

They lie to get what they want.

So call me a pessimist when it comes to love, but I've got good data to back up my conclusions.

Still, my friends have all fallen in love, and despite my own feelings on the matter, I want to support them. I'm totally determined to be the ultra-cool aunt to Evie and Kayla's kids (and may have already designed awesome onesies for each one to wear home from the hospital) and eventually Lauren and Shelby's too.

"So what do you guys think of this one?" Shelby nudges my shoulder and I turn to face the pregnant crowd. "You can trade out the top for whatever style you want, which is a fun option."

Evie and Kayla coo their approval just as Lauren emerges from the dressing room, her deep red dress trailing a short train behind her. The color complements her skin tone perfectly and, combined with her long hair and high cheekbones, she's positively regal—an appropriate thing since she's marrying the prince of Kentonia next spring.

"Isn't this one the bomb?" she squeals. "Sooooo gorgeous!"

I have to grin, because as soon as she speaks, she

sounds nothing like a stuffy princess. I'm so glad she hasn't let the fame or new position change her.

Shelby's eyes fill with tears and she takes Lauren's hands. "*You* are gorgeous. You're totally going to upstage me if you wear this dress. All of you will."

Knowing Shelby, hearing the awe in her sweet voice, that would be okay. She's on the quiet side, with a considerate nature that leaves everyone feeling calmer in her presence. But ever since she started dating her best friend Eric and starred in her school's production of *Cinderella* a few months ago, I've noticed she doesn't seem quite as keen to stay in the shadows. She never seeks out the spotlight, but she also doesn't seem to mind it like she used to. I'm proud of the way she's started speaking up and sharing her opinions.

But I'll still step in and be bossy when needed. Like right now.

"First of all, not true. No one is going to upstage the bride." I purse my lips at her. "But if you feel that way, then no dice. Looks like we're wearing this monstrosity." Waving my hands over my body, I throw a sassy look her way.

"That dress is gorgeous too." Lauren saunters over and slings an arm around my shoulders. "*Monstrosity.* You're hilarious, Lexi Lou."

I remain stoic, stiff, because I'm not someone who likes to be touched. But also, my dad used to call me variations of Lexi, and Lauren's insistent use of the nickname always rubs a little salt in that wound. Of course, she knows nothing about that wound, because I haven't told any of my friends about my dad. It's just her way of showing me her love.

That's what nicknames *should* be—an outward expression of your inward affection. But there will always be those who take what should be good and twist them. I thought my dad loved me when he called me Lexi Boo, Lexi Roo, Lexi Bell. But if he'd loved me, he never would have gotten on that airplane the day he died.

Then there's Dax and his obnoxious nickname he uses purely to annoy me. He's—

Argh. No. I shake off the thought because it's bad enough he takes up brain space during work hours. He can't have this time too.

Schooling my features into one of nonchalance, I ask Shelby, "Which dress do *you* like better? I'm sure there are more options if you want us to keep trying." Not that I want to. But again. I'd do anything for my friends.

Lauren sighs and lays her head on my shoulder since we're about the same height. "Options. What would that be like? So far, I've been told the date I'm getting married, the dress I'm wearing, the color of the flowers, the venue, and basically everything except which underwear I have to put on the day of. And knowing her, that will probably be dictated by Ms. Flutterbum too." She crosses her eyes and sticks out her tongue as she purposefully mispronounces the name of Kentonia's royal wedding coordinator, Felicia Butterflum.

"Cheer up, mate." Kayla holds a Dorito in the air. "At least you get to pick your bridesmaids."

"Barely," Lauren mutters. "They're trying to get me to take on Topher's fourth cousin, Lavinia. Did you know that it's even possible to have a fourth cousin? When do we stop counting? Fifth? Seventeenth? I've already got his sister as a bridesmaid—though I would have asked Chloe anyway—and his second cousin's daughter as the flower girl. Topher's never even met the mom but 'her little Poinsettia will be adorable in curls and the frilliest dress we can find.'" Her voice turns high-pitched and British-like at the end as she imitates Ms. Butterflum.

"Well"—I hip bump her—"you also got to pick the groom. Though if you choose to back out of this whole ordeal and stay put right here in San Diego with us, we'd all support you."

"Boo!" Kayla chucks a chip at me, but it lands pitifully at Evie's feet.

Evie tries to lean forward to pick it up. But thanks to her belly acting as a barrier, she only succeeds in moving about an inch, stretching her hands outward like a T-rex with short stumpy arms. It's quite the sight, and the three of us on stage can't help but break down into giggles.

"Oh, sure, laugh at the pregnant lady," Evie says, a good-natured grin on her face.

"Leave it, Evs." Kayla throws her head back dramatically. "Preserve what little dignity you have left."

"*Is* there any left?"

"Oh, yes, girl. We haven't given birth yet, and that's sure to suck all dignity from our bone marrow. Nothing like exposing your goods for the world to see."

"Or, you know, just the doctor and a few nurses."

Evie grabs another chip from the bag and frowns. "Aw, man. Last one."

Shelby titters her adorable little laugh, then turns to face both Lauren and me, tapping her delicate chin. "Okay, okay. I really love Lauren's, but I think for a summer wedding in Hallmark Beach, Alexis's is perfect. Evie and Kayla, you can get a top that makes nursing more accessible, and Alexis, Deb, and Lauren can select the top that makes them feel the most like themselves."

"Does it come in T-shirt style?" I tease.

"I'll ask." Shelby winks, eyes sparkling. I hate to admit what love has done for her, but I'm not an idiot. Finally being able to express what she feels for Eric—and having his support and love in return—has changed her for the better. She'd be completely whole and lovely on her own, but some people are made to be wives and moms. Shelby is definitely one of them.

All of my friends are.

And I'm destined to have a cat. Maybe three. Woohoo.

"Yay! Decision made." Kayla lumbers to her feet and holds out her hands toward Evie. "Now we can go eat something. I'm starving."

"We literally just ate an entire bag of chips." Evie glances askance at the empty Doritos bag and takes Kayla's hands, using them as leverage to stand. "But yeah, I could go for some pizza. You ladies in?"

Shelby stifles a yawn. "I don't know. I have to be at work kind of early."

"Same," Lauren says. "They've got me teaching the 5 a.m. spin class. But I'm contemplating just not going to bed tonight, teaching my classes, and then sleeping the rest of the day tomorrow."

"You just want an excuse to not be available when Flutterbum calls to talk wedding deets." I arch my eyebrows, daring her to argue.

"Guilty as charged."

We all laugh, and my friends turn to me.

"Alexis?" Evie asks.

"Sure." I tug at a loose thread on the bodice of my dress, remembering just in time to not pull at the snag since this isn't mine. "After the day I had, you'd better throw in a pitcher of beer too."

"A whole pitcher?" Kayla grunts, probably over the fact she can't drink for a few more months. "What happened today?"

"Nothing I want to go into." Because every time I mention Dax—

"Did *Dax* happen today?" Kayla's bottom lip twitches and her eyes fill with mirth.

Yep, there it is. My friends don't seem to understand that Dax Nyhart is Enemy Numero Uno. He's Thanos and Malekith and Justin Hammer and the Green Goblin all rolled into one. Much more attractive, I'll give them that. But looks have only ever been deceiving.

I fix my glare on Kayla, who is far too perceptive for her own good. Not that it would take a genius to decipher what might have occurred to put me in a mood. But still. "I don't want to talk about it." I spin on my heel and head to the dressing room, where my hand gets tangled in the curtain when I attempt to toss it out of my way.

My heart rate is high stepping, taking my blood vessels for a ride, and I close the curtain with a jerk before resting my head against the wall of the dressing room. My friends don't understand.

Then again, how could they? I've never told them the full truth of things.

Them? They're open books. I know almost everything about them—partly because I'm observant, but also because they share so freely.

I wish I could be like that, fully open and vulnerable. I am with Kennedy. Mostly. But that's because she knows my past. She's part of it. We have that pain, that betrayal, in common. And thank the stars, instead of seeing the other as an enemy—like we very well could have—we found in each other an ally. A friend. A constant.

Shimmying out of the gown, I quickly dress and head back to my friends. They're all standing in a closed circle, even Lauren, who's back in her pink yoga pants and black workout tank.

Watching them laugh as Kayla acts out some hilarious story about one of her dating coach clients, there's this niggle of something tight behind my ribs. It pokes and prods my heart, attempting to gain entrance. But I know I can't let it in, can't let myself fully feel it.

Because no matter how much I love these ladies like sisters, like the family I never had, the truth of the matter is that they're all moving on from me. In their own ways, each one is on a new path headed toward a bright future filled with love and joy.

I want that for them. Seriously.

But I can't bear to let myself think about what happens when Shelby gets married next summer and sets up house with Eric. When Lauren moves across the ocean to Europe and marries Topher. When Evie and Kayla's babies are born and they become consumed with diapers and breastfeeding and playdates and sleep schedules.

How did I get myself into this mess in the first place? I'd been doing so well, keeping everyone but Kennedy at arm's length. But then I put out that stupid ad for housemates nearly a decade ago ... and the rest is history.

I tug at my braid and the physical discomfort in my scalp is a reminder. There's nothing I can do to stop my friends from leaving. All I can do? Redouble my determination, my efforts, to become financially independent. Sure, I could try to find new roommates, but I can't risk that. I got lucky with four amazing housemates the first time, but I'm not one to tempt fate a second time.

Besides, I have no desire to get close to new roommates only to lose them again.

Which means, for now, working with Dax.

Stars above, help me.

"All right, people." I charge forward, breaking up the happy little circle. "We going to eat or what?"

two

. . .

"WELL, if it isn't my protégé."

At Dax's ever-grating voice, my chin tips up and I find him leaning against my office's door jamb the next morning, his hair full and styled, hands in the pockets of his pressed black trousers. Today he's wearing a burgundy sweater over a dark green button-up, and I briefly wonder what the occasion is. Maybe he's got a date night with Lilith.

Not that I care.

"Come to gloat?"

"Me?" He places a hand on his well-defined chest (what? Objectively it IS well-defined) and his eyes feign innocence. "I would never. Just popping by to tell you how thrilled I am to be helping out." His grin is as wide as the Grand Canyon and I've never wanted to smack a look off someone's face as badly as I do right now.

I wrinkle my nose at him, like he's stinking up my space. (Ugh, if only. Why does *Eau de Jerk* smell so delectable?) "Yes, thanks for showing me the ropes that I've been climbing for a lot longer than you. Appreciate it."

If his chuckle is any indication, he's not offended in the least at my sarcasm. In fact, he chooses to step more fully into my office, shutting the door behind him.

I lift an eyebrow. "What are you doing?"

"Having our first team meeting. You mind?"

"Do you really want me to answer that?"

Dax grabs my extra chair, swings it around, and sits in it backward. Then he proceeds to stare at me. I stare back. His head tilts, eyes softening just a tad, then squinting as if trying to make something out. The buzz of one of my fluorescent lights, the kick of the heater, the distant traffic coming from four stories down ... these sounds fill the space between us.

Dax's always-present grin is gone, and in its place his lips flatten out. They're neither extremely plump nor thin, but somewhere in between.

Why are you thinking about his lips, Alexis?

"Well?" My rough voice breaks the silence.

"I overheard your talk with my uncle yesterday."

His uncle. He never refers to Nate as anything but "the boss." Interesting that he would choose to change that now. To emphasize their relationship. "Eavesdropping is rude."

He wiggles his fingers at the wall behind him. "Not if it's unintentional."

"Always an excuse." Holding in a sigh, I realize my voice lacks conviction. There's not much fight left in me today. I'm tired from staying out way too late, there's a headache lingering from the buzz of the alcohol I drank last night, and my heart kind of feels … sore. Assaulted. I just want to go home, kick up my feet, and get lost in a sci-fi novel. Maybe a movie. I'm not sure I'll have enough brain power left after this "meeting" to do anything but veg.

"In this case, maybe it's a good thing I overheard." He glances up at the ceiling, then back at me. "For what it's worth, I think Nate is out of line. You don't need my help."

What? I cross my arms over my chest, narrow my eyes at him. "Really." What's his angle?

"Yeah, really." His lips bend into that crooked smile girls must go crazy over. Other girls. Not me, sir. "You're beyond help."

My fingers find a pen and I wind back to toss it at him, when he puts his hands up in front of his face and laughs. "I'm kidding, RB. Put down the weapon."

But I keep it at eye level. "No."

He must hear the challenge in my voice because he suddenly stands and rounds my desk, pulling the pen from my hand before I have a chance to move. Then he slips it into his pocket.

"Hey! That's mine." I start to reach for it, then think better of that idea, considering its placement.

At my reaction, Dax's idiotic grin floats over me. He thinks he's won. But that pen is mine and I'll get it back sooner or later.

"Well, as productive as this 'meeting' has been—"

"I actually had a thought about Nate's plan," he says.

I stand, because I hate feeling shorter than others. I'm the average height of a woman, but Dax has at least six inches on me. This once again puts us uncomfortably close, but to step back would be to admit defeat. "That we should … what? Follow it?"

"Not exactly."

Huh. "Okay, I'm listening."

"It's just, yesterday you sounded kind of …" He shrugs. "I don't know. Desperate to get some of the bigger accounts. Guess I'm wondering why."

And suddenly, the heater's pumping out waves of warmth that are making my palms sweat. "That's not any of your business." I finally step back, slide down into my chair once more, and flick my chin in the direction of the other chair—a reminder of whose office this is and who is in charge.

Apparently he understands my gesturing and walks around the desk, flipping the chair back the way it should be and then sinking into it. "Yeah, I know it's not. You're right." Scratching behind his ear, he clears his throat. "All right, it's like this. I have a proposition for you."

What could he possibly have to propose? "I'm sorry?" The ending of the last word tips upward and goes breathy.

Dax shakes his head. "Get your mind out of the gutter, RB. Nothing like that." He taps his chin. "Though now that you mention it—"

Ugh, gross. "I didn't."

"Now that you've thought it—"

"Didn't do that either." My front teeth cement together.

"Now that it's out there ..."

At my death glare, he chuckles. "Kidding, kidding. But seriously, I do have something to ask you. A favor of sorts."

"Why would I do you a favor? You've done nothing but make my work life a living—"

"Watch your language there, RB."

"I was going to say 'dream.'" I completely deadpan, sarcasm falling like drool from my lips.

"Right, right. Naturally." A chuckle, a pause. "All right, before I tell you what I need, I'm going to tell you what you stand to gain. If you do this for me, I'll give you your pick of my accounts. Whichever three you want. We wouldn't even have to do any official training."

So far this is sounding good. Too good. "Don't you think dear old Uncle Nate would notice our lack of meetings and training?"

"Not really, but if you're worried, we can pretend to meet. Or we can exchange tips—I'm sure there's stuff you can teach me."

I snort. "Oh, yeah?"

"Yeah." He removes my pen from his pocket and clicks it a few times. "Like how to get my hair such a bright purple color."

Note to self: change hair color tonight.

He continues. "Or how to insult people with a single glare."

I eye the pen, willing it to fly toward me like I'm

Hermione Granger without the wand. "And what would you want in exchange for this very generous offer?"

He stops clicking, tilts his head. "It IS generous, isn't it?"

Oh, the man is infuriating. Must he have a remark or retort for everything I say? "I'm about to get up and walk out of here, so you'd better get on with it." I jut out my hand, wait.

He holds my gaze for one, two, three, then leans forward and slips the pen into my palm. A peace offering. Huh. He must really need me to do this favor for him.

Which begs the question—why me?

"I'll be honest. I was already trying to figure out a way to ask you this, but you needing something in return makes me feel better about it."

"Okay, what in the world do you want from me? This is starting to sound a bit … Um …"

"Scandalous?" His gaze finds mine and I can't help the way my toes curl at the look in them. Something dark and deep and … wanting.

But no, I'm reading him wrong, because in the next instance, he's laughing again. "Nothing like that, though it is a bit, shall we say, unorthodox."

"Dax, I swear. If you don't spit it out—"

"I need you to pretend to be my fiancée."

If it's possible to sway while sitting, pretty sure I just did that. "What?" I clear the sudden frog in my throat. "W-why?"

Standing, the man starts pacing. "It's like this, all

right? I applied for another job, one at a family-centric toy company in Los Angeles. They're looking for an internal marketing director. It's a dream job, really. Pay raise. Some travel, but not too much. And best of all, not working for my uncle."

I sit up straight. Why wouldn't he want to work for his uncle? He's got it made here at Birmingham & Co. If I didn't know any better, I'd think Nate was grooming him to take over the business one day—a not-so-happy thought, indeed.

I must not do a very good job containing my surprise, because Dax nods. "I know, Nate's been great, but I've got to stand on my own two feet. It's time. And you'd be happy, right? Not only would I be out of your hair—in another city—but if I get this job, I'll recommend that you get all of my accounts. All of them, Alexis."

All of them. I do some quick mental calculations and wow. With the kinds of bonuses that would provide, I'd definitely have enough money to pay off my house before Shelby and Lauren move out. I might even have enough to help Kennedy go back to school, if that's what she wants to do. Last I checked, she blew all of her inheritance in a matter of months, much of it on that worthless boyfriend.

Focus, Alexis. A dream job, he said. Sounds like a dream to me—to be free of Dax Nyhart.

But wait. "So what does this have to do with me pretending to be ..." A shudder grips my spine. I can't even think it. The very idea is completely ludicrous. Abominable. Comical.

I catch Dax's eye. He's watching me with an expression I've never seen. A guarded one. He always pretends to be so open, but right now, he's hiding something.

Is it something nefarious? Or maybe just … pain?

No, no. Dax is just as shallow as he's always been. There's nothing new here, except that he's approaching me for a favor. Not that I'd ever in a million years agree to this. It's asinine. Pretending to be his fiancée would mean lying. And probably holding his hand.

Even …

No. I'd never contemplate kissing *him* of all people.

My face warms. Darn heater. I finish my earlier question. "… your fiancée?"

"Yeah, um, so when I initially interviewed for the job—like three months ago—I mentioned my fiancée. They seemed to like that I was engaged, was about to be a family man. They're seriously into that image and want to hire people who fit it to a T."

That seems strange to me, but to each his own, I suppose.

"And they finally contacted me yesterday for a second-round interview, but they … well, they want us to meet for dinner." He leans forward. "And they asked me to bring my fiancée."

"That's super strange. Why?"

"Said they feel like the whole family would be committing to work there, and the whole office would be committing to me—and a huge part of my life is the woman I love." He clears his throat. "One of the owners told me outright that they're considering two candidates, and the other guy is already married with three kids. But he quote-unquote 'likes what I have to offer.' So if this interview goes well, I think I'd have a good chance of getting the job."

My head is kind of spinning, and I blink as I try to take in the details of what he's told me. I want to ask more about this company and their weird priorities, but there's another more pressing question at the forefront of my mind. "So why are you asking me? I mean, I know this sounds crazy, but why don't you ask your *real* fiancée to go? What's her name? Lilac? Daisy? Rose?"

"Lilith. And we broke up." He shrugs, runs a hand through his perfect crop of hair. I wonder what it would feel like beneath my fingers.

WHAT?! No, you do NOT wonder that, Alexis Marie Matkin. Because he's your nemesis, or did you forget?

But wait, what did he say? They broke up? I cross my arms over my chest, lift an eyebrow. "Got sick of you, did she? I really can't say I blame her."

He smiles, but something quivers in his gaze. Almost like I've hit a nerve.

And I'm tempted to feel bad. I probably should. Okay, maybe I do. But I definitely can't let him see that. He'll exploit any weakness I have. Because that's what men do.

"You're a real charmer, you know, that Rainbow Brite?" He chuckles like he's soooo clever.

Argh. "We get it. My hair is colorful. Find a new joke."

Amusement lights to life in his eyes. "That's not why I call you Rainbow Brite."

I roll my eyes. "Sure, it's not."

"Really."

He has me a tiny bit intrigued. I lift an eyebrow. "Okay. Why then?"

No one's teeth should be as white as his when he grins. He probably uses those whitening strips like the prima donna he is.

Although he's a very handsome prima donna ...

Shut up, stupid subconscious. "Well?"

"I call you Rainbow Brite ..." He leans in just a tad bit more, and I find the air between us vibrates. How annoying. Even the air is enamored with him.

But not me. I can see right through his games.

Despite myself, I lean forward a fraction of an inch as well.

"Nah, I don't think you're ready to hear it." Dax straightens. "And I can tell you're not ready to make a decision about this yet either. I'll leave you to think about it. But you don't have long. The dinner is next Friday night."

Standing, he slips his hands into his pockets and walks out the door, whistling. Then he backtracks, sticking his head inside my office once more. "By the way, this offer won't last forever. Just let me know you're in before I find another partner."

"You mean victim."

He either doesn't hear me or chooses to ignore me, because he continues his jaunty tune like he doesn't have a care in the world—which, he apparently does, given he has to either come clean about his newfound single status or risk losing the prospective job. Then he winks at me before his face disappears and the door shuts behind him.

Chucking my pen at the door, I clench my fists. That man is so … argh! I want him gone. Pronto. He's too flirtatious—too charismatic—for his own good. For *my* own good.

And let me clarify: It's because he keeps stealing the good accounts, NOT because I personally am attracted to him. The fact that he is now single also plays no bearing on my desire to see him gone-zo.

If only I could do something to get him out of here—something that *wouldn't* require me to pretend to be in love with him.

three

THE WEEKEND HAS FLOWN by in a haze. I'm sitting here, alone, on my bright blue couch. It's Sunday evening and the clock is ticking closer and closer to bedtime.

Sundays just before bed are the worst time of the week.

Shelby is still out with Eric, though I expect her home soon. The last time I checked, Lauren was in her room talking to Topher even though it's super late in Kentonia. But he works almost all day every day, and his only real time to chat is at night, which suits Lauren since she's a night owl.

Funny. I never thought I'd have so much in common with a prince, but I've spent most of my weekend working too, trying to come up with a better design for Adolf's coffee filters, each one worse than the last. (The latest iteration features a yippy dog with half an ear and a quote bubble saying "We don't need no stinking coffee"—so, yeah. That's where I'm at.)

At this point, I'm firmly convinced that Nate is going to fire my butt, or at least demote me. (To what? No idea, since there isn't really a "junior brand manager.") I've come to the conclusion that there's absolutely no way that I can turn this account around on my own. The reality is that Adolf is probably going to find a new digital marketing company to work with—or request to be reassigned to a different brand manager.

And that would be fine with me. For real. But that would also be a sure signal to Nate that I'm not ready for the big leagues. There's literally no way to convince him without Dax's say-so. And working with *him*? Torture.

Unless I didn't actually work with him. But that would require …

No! I will not pretend to be engaged to him. I—

My phone buzzes on the coffee table and I pull my feet out from under my lime-green blanket, lean forward, snag it, answer. Kennedy's face appears on the screen. My baby sister's brown, highlighted hair flows around her shoulders, and her eyes are a cool shade of lavender. The bronzer on her cheeks is applied to perfection, and while I can only see her from the collarbone up, I catch a glimpse of the gold cross necklace her mom gave her on her eighteenth birthday, not long before she died.

"Hey," I say.

She squints. "Why is it so dark there?"

"Sorry." Reaching for the fan remote, I click on the

overhead light. I love this living room. My aunt left behind most of the furniture when she moved out, and between the patchwork chair, abstract art, and the most comfortable couch ever, I found that her eclectic style suited me quite well. It's possible I feel more myself here than anywhere. "That better?"

"Your hair is orange." It's a statement, not a question. "I thought you were going to leave it purple for at least a week this time."

I shrug and curl my legs back underneath me, pulling the blanket taut. "Decided I needed a change."

"I wore my colored contacts so we'd match." Her bottom lip protrudes, a pout that has softened me toward her from the very moment we met at our father's funeral—her as an adorable and confused four-year-old hiding under a table and me as the equally confused thirteen-year-old who found her and scooted underneath to comfort her before realizing exactly who she was.

The other woman's daughter.

His daughter.

My half-sister.

"Sorry, Ken. You know I like to change things up on the regular."

She giggles and reclines against the dark-blue duvet that covers the bed she shares with her boyfriend, holding the phone above her. "You sound so old when you talk like that. Nobody says 'on the regular' anymore."

I roll my eyes and smile. "We can't all be as hip as you, Miss Social Media Influencer."

Her grin seriously could go on billboards if she ever had any interest in modeling. And it's not surprising. Our dad was a good-looking guy, but her mother was Julia Roberts-level gorgeous. Kennedy won the genetics lottery, that's for sure.

Not only is she beautiful, but killer smart to boot. If she had put any amount of effort into college, she could have aced it. Instead, she turned to partying, drinking away her inheritance (at least from our dad's side—her mom's mom is still holding on to a huge trust fund she will give Kennedy "when she's responsible enough") until she dropped out a few years ago. She started wait-ressing at a high-end bar up in San Francisco, and that's when she met Brooks.

She stretches and yawns. Her "job" keeps her up late. I don't pretend to understand the kind of life she's carved out for herself, but I do know that I worry about her. "Well, what's new with you? Did you have a good weekend?" she asks.

"I worked."

"So, nothing new then." Kennedy clucks her tongue. "You have got to find a way to start enjoying life, big sister."

"We can't all live off of our boyfriend and random people on the Internet." Ooo. Too far. I know it before I see her crumpled brow. "Sorry. I didn't mean that."

"Yes, you did. I get it. You're the responsible one, and I'm just the mooch, right?"

I groan and sink down against the arm of the couch. "That's not what I said. But I do wish you'd move down here again. Brooks isn't good for you."

Upon first meeting him, Kennedy's boyfriend seems as smooth as they come. He's slick and shiny, like a new car off the lot—but one with mechanical defects you can't see on the surface. He's always dressed to the nines, a byproduct of his job as a big-city attorney, and image is clearly very important to him. Case in point: he won't even take a picture with Kennedy unless her hair and makeup are done.

Yeah, that's right. HER hair and makeup.

As a social media influencer, she claims to understand, spews some garbage about the importance of always looking her best, but I hate how she is around Brooks. Being in a relationship should make each person better. Just like with Shelby, it should puff people up, bring out their strengths. But when Kennedy is around Brooks, my vivacious—albeit impulsive—twenty-three-year-old sister becomes much smaller, bending and bowing to whatever her live-in boyfriend of two years wants.

Being nine years older, it's my job to protect her from jerks like that. Maybe I should have ignored her protests and moved with her when she left San Diego for school in San Francisco five years ago. It's not like I haven't thought about doing it still, especially now that my roommates will all be leaving. But even if I sold my house and made a tidy profit here, the cost of living in the Bay area is astronomical.

Plus, Kennedy wouldn't want me butting into her life.

So I settle for our weekly Sunday night chats, a time when I'm free to check in without seeming too overbearing. Though, given the look she's searing me with right now, I apparently have crossed even that line.

Thankfully, she never holds a grudge for long. It's one of the things I love about her—how easily she forgives. (On the other hand, it does mean she stays with Brooks even when he's a complete donkey to her.)

She rolls over onto her stomach and props the phone against what I assume are her pillows, then places her chin on her folded hands flat on the mattress. "Alexis, we really need to get you a boyfriend so you stop obsessing about my love life." The tease in her tone is nothing new, but I sense the serious undertones in what she's saying.

"You know where I stand on that matter."

"All men are pigs, yada yada." Her eyes radiate warmth, and other than their unnatural color, they remind me so much of our dad's, it hurts. "You're going to have to open your heart one of these days, you know."

I fiddle with the edge of the blanket and trace an infinity symbol into the long fibers. "I don't get it, Ken."

"What?"

"How you can trust so freely after what Dad did."

She sighs, her pretty bow-shaped lips tipping down. "I think it's just my natural inclination. But also, I barely knew him. And he … we …" My sister bites her bottom lip. "Well, you know."

Yeah, I do. She and her mom weren't the family who was betrayed. She wasn't the daughter who begged her father to find a job where he didn't have to "travel" fifty percent of the time, who had to watch him constantly fly away claiming he was doing what was necessary to support her and her mother.

Granted, neither Pippa nor my mom knew the other existed, so there *was* a betrayal. But it still isn't the same—to be the ones chosen because his first family wasn't enough.

Something pulses behind my eyes and my nostrils start to itch. I need to steer this conversation elsewhere, pronto. "Oh, speaking of work, I have something equal parts funny and horrifying to tell you about."

Kennedy blinks and it takes a second, but she sits up on her elbows. "Yeah? What?"

So I tell her about Adolf ("he sounds like a winner!") and then Nate ("oh no, he didn't!"). Then I get to the cream of the story—the part I know will have her in stitches, because she's totally one of those women who loves reality TV and yet also recognizes the utter ridiculousness of it.

"And then Dax, get this, asked me to be his fake fiancée for this interview!" I pause for effect, waiting for the laugh that never comes. "Ken, did you hear me?" Maybe the connection froze, because she's just staring at me. But no, she's blinking. "Ken?"

"Processing." She holds up a finger and moves her swoop bangs to the right side of her face. "Okay, got it. So what did you say to him?"

"Really, I expected more of a reaction from you of all people." I push my hand through my thick hair, which is in desperate need of a wash after being piled on my head all weekend. "I didn't really give him an answer one way or the other, but isn't the answer obvious?"

"So you're doing it, then?"

"What? No!"

"Oh." A pause. She turns her head to the side, then covers the phone and says something in muted tones. Finally, her face appears again. "Sorry, Brooks is home and he wants me to get ready for dinner."

"I thought you were exhausted."

She puts on a weary grin. "Gotta have something memorable to post about tomorrow. Plus you know he likes to cash in on my free restaurant eats, and he's been working all weekend."

Since it will do absolutely no good, I hold back my thoughts on that subject. "So wait, before you go … you think I should do it? Pretend to be the fiancée of the man I loathe?"

"What better way to get rid of him than to help ensure he gets a job somewhere else?"

"But I hate lying." Loathe it more than I loathe Dax. I think. Or do I? Maybe I could get on board with a little white lie if it means everything else falls into place. Ugh. I hate moral ambiguity.

"Look, Alexis, I know you have your principles and that's all well and good. But sometimes you just have to take a risk, you know? What's the big deal? You go to dinner, spend a few hours with him, help convince these people he's perfect for the job—that's not lying since you DO think it's perfect for him to be far away from you, right?"

Well, when she puts it like that, it doesn't sound quite so terrible. Still … "I don't really see how it would work. All the details. Like, what are his expectations, for one thing? And do I have to dress up? Because that might be a dealbreaker."

"Which one?" Kennedy laughs.

"Both, actually."

"You don't know? So ask him." Kennedy sits up, looks again toward her doorway, back at me. "I've gotta go. Brooks is hungry. Love you. Text me what you decide."

"Okay. Love—"

But she hangs up before I can finish. Stupid Brooks and his hunger pangs.

My butt went numb about ten minutes ago, so I yank the blanket off and stand, my muscles protesting the sudden movement. After wiggling my toes and feet, I penguin walk to the back door and slide it open.

Stars cloak the sky, but wispy clouds create a hazy film over it all. A cool breeze dances across my skin, raising goosebumps on my upper arms. The world is so vast, the universe so wide and deep, that this tiny decision of mine shouldn't matter, shouldn't torment me. But don't they say that a butterfly beating its wings can theoretically cause ripples around the world?

And right now, I don't have all the factors necessary to make a decision about whether to go along with Dax's kooky plan.

"*So ask him.*" Kennedy's urging nudges my memory.

Oh, what the heck. I open my phone, find his contact information—which I have purely because we work at a tiny company, and Nate insists we all have multiple ways to get ahold of one another—and hit the call button before I can stop myself.

"Hey, RB. Fancy hearing from you on a Sunday evening. I was just thinking about you."

I don't have time for pleasantries—or nonsense. "Why me?"

"Why was I thinking about you?" His voice is low, slightly husky. Teasing. "Oh, let me count the reasons."

"No, not that." I shake out my jittery legs. "Why did you ask me to be your fake fiancée when I clearly don't like you?"

"Ouch. That hurts, RB." But his tone tells me he's not really offended. He's enjoying this.

I walk out into the small backyard and begin to pace, my bare feet cold in the grass. "I'm going to hang up if you can't be serious."

"All right, all right. Chill." A pause. "I asked the great Alexis Matkin because you, of all people, won't think anything more of it than what it is—a business transaction." He clears his throat. "I'm not looking to get involved with anyone again for a long time and I would hate to lead a woman on."

Oh. Wow. A bit of true honesty from him. Didn't expect that. "Well, good. Me either. I'm not looking to get involved with anyone, that is."

"So … is that a yes?"

I'm going to regret this, aren't I? "It's more like an I'll-agree-to-your-terms-but-if-you-touch-me-I'll-murder-you."

He coughs. "Good to know where you stand." A pause. "You do know we will probably have to touch, though, right? At least a little bit, or it won't come off as real. And if you want to get rid of me for good, then you're going to have to be at least somewhat convincing."

Some sort of bug crawls across my big toe and I suppress a squeal while hightailing it back to the concrete. "I get it. Fine. But no funny business or you'll lose a finger. Possibly the whole arm. Do I make myself clear?"

"Maybe we need to talk particulars so I don't risk loss of life *or* limb." His tone titters, and I can tell he thinks I'm being over the top. But if we are doing this, *I'm* going to be the one controlling the situation, not him.

Another question pops into my mind. "So what happens if you get the job? You're going to have to tell your new crew eventually that we aren't together anymore."

"You mean you don't actually want to end up marrying me?"

My jaw drops. I thought I'd been clear, but—

"I'm kidding, Alexis. I can hear your freakout from here."

Right. "I knew that."

"Uh huh." Warm, smooth chuckles vibrate across the airwaves and into my very bones. "I'll wait a few months and then let them know we broke up. A mutual split. Irreconcilable differences."

"I'll say," I mutter under my breath.

"What's that?"

"Nothing." I shiver as the breeze picks up and bites into me now. "So ..."

"So."

"Okay, then. Guess I'll see you Friday."

He laughs. "Guess I'll see you tomorrow. You know, at work."

"Right. Yeah, of course." Why am I so flustered right now? Probably still a reaction to that bug on my foot. I do *not* like bugs. "You can give me the details about Friday sometime this week. Do we have to go to Los Angeles?"

"Nope. They said they've been looking for an excuse to use their San Diego beach house."

So they're rich. "Sounds good."

"Yep."

"Okay then." And I stand there, like a weirdo, just waiting. "Um, bye, I guess."

"Good night, RB. Sleep tight. Don't let the bed bugs bite."

I click off the call without another word, shivering at his mention of bugs. I don't know what it is about this scheme of his that has me jumpy. But I have a feeling I'm going to have a perpetual case of the creepy-crawlies all week until Friday night is over and done with.

four

. . .

"ALEXIS, good, you're here. I want to chat."

Those are the first words I hear upon walking into the office on Thursday morning. I pull up short at the sight of Nate standing beside Gina's desk. Am I late or something? But a quick peek at the clock on the wall shows that, no, it's eight-thirty-two, and Nate's never been a stickler for a few minutes here or there. A few of the Drs. Strange aren't even at their desks yet, so that can't be why Nate wants to talk with me.

"Sure, yeah." Gripping the straps of my backpack purse, I ignore Gina's tight-lipped acknowledgment and plunge through the quiet hallways. We pass the small break room, where one of the good Drs. is chatting up Penelope in front of the coffee machine. I catch a whiff of the horrid stuff and grimace.

Once we reach Nate's office, he waits for me before shutting the door behind me. "Please, take a seat."

I remove my backpack and place it on my lap as I

lower myself into a chair. His office is bigger than mine, but his cherrywood desk and bookcases take up most of the space. "Is everything okay?"

I really don't need any more bad news. This week has not been a great one. The expected happened on Monday when Adolf requested to be placed with another brand manager and Nate assigned him to Rupert. (Who, consequently, uses and loves Jonesing's coffee filters, and can handle grumps because he is one —so it's a win-win for both of them. Not so much for me.)

Nate leans forward from behind his desk, the patched elbows of his tweed jacket creeping back up his arm. "Just wanted to see how things are going with Dax."

Oh. "Um. Yeah. Okay, I guess." *Please don't ask particulars.*

He thinks Dax and I have been meeting this week to work on Dax's client projects. I *have* been helping him— giving my suggestions for improvement, him arguing with me about why that won't work (and doing so in the most annoying arrogant way possible)—but our "meetings" haven't been anything except quick check-ins. Even that is more interaction than we've had before, and each one is more grating than the last. I think if we had to meet for longer than five minutes, one of us might honestly kill the other. (On second thought, I'd definitely kill him. He seems to get a sick sort of plea-sure out of making me mad.)

Thankfully, Dax hasn't mentioned the elephant in the room that's been stomping on my lungs ever since

Sunday night. But we're going to have to talk about tomorrow night eventually.

"Great." Nate's face relaxes. I hadn't even caught on that his eyebrows had bunched together, his forehead creased, until I see the tension leave him, but now it's obvious. "I know you didn't like the idea, but I really do think you can learn a lot from him."

Just drive the knife in deeper there, Nate. "Mmm hmm," I murmur, because what else is there to say? "Speaking of meetings, I've got one soon. So …?"

He claps, leans back in his chair. "Right, yes. Go ahead. Just wanted to make sure my dream team was making it happen."

Dream team. Ha. "We so are." I try—really I do—to keep the sarcasm from my tone, but I'm afraid it's tinged with it. Maybe even saturated. Better get out of here before he notices. "Thanks." I stand.

His phone rings and he waves at me as he answers. I take the opportunity to dart down the hallway to my office, the door of which is standing open even though I close it every night before I leave.

And there's Dax sitting on the edge of my desk, arms crossed over his broad chest like he doesn't have anything better to do. He smiles at me, something mischievous in the grin. "Oh, hey, RB. Fancy seeing you here."

Ugh, why is he so chipper in the mornings? The guy just likes to hear himself talk, I think. "Why are you in my office before I am?"

"Waiting for you, of course."

"Move." I swat at him and when he doesn't remove

his rear from my desk, I push his arm—unintentionally grabbing his bicep. Oh my goodness, it's solid. And large. Whatever. He wants to sit on my desk? Let him. I round the desk and plop into my chair, stowing my purse in the bottom drawer of my desk. "What do you want?"

Laughing, he hops down and swivels to face me. "You're a morning person, aren't you?"

Glaring at him, I notice my stack of Post-It Notes has been moved from one side of my desk to the other. I move it back. "You're so childish. And annoying."

"It's just so fun to rile you."

"Oh, you don't want to see me truly riled."

"Maybe I do."

His teasing flirtation pricks into my armor, but I shake it off. "Believe me. You really don't."

"Agree to disagree. Love the green hair, by the way. I think Jeremy won the pool this week."

"Pool?" And who is Jeremy? Oh, maybe one of the Drs. Strange.

"Yeah, we all take bets on what color your hair is going to be the next week."

Seriously? "Don't you all have lives?"

"Yes, lives made more entertaining by your revolving door of colors." He places a hand over his heart. "Don't you feel good knowing you've made all of our lives brighter, RB? And I do mean that in the most literal sense."

"I don't do this for anyone else but me." I started dying my hair in high school as a way to stand out, be different. To be anyone other than the me I'd been …

before. But my preppy boarding school only allowed blondes, reds, browns, and blacks—"natural" colors—so when I graduated, I took my hair color to another level. Purples, oranges, greens, blues. No color is off-limits now.

Except that basic brown color my hair was when I was naive. Innocent. Before I knew that men could tell you one thing and mean another. That they might say they loved you, but their love wasn't true. Now, I'm fully me. Fully colored, by the world, by reality.

And I'll never go back.

So the fact that something that means so much to me —that represents something I put my heart into—has become a point of entertainment for others makes me want to scream. But I won't give Dax the satisfaction of knowing that.

Maybe if I ignore him, he'll leave.

I turn to my computer and open my email program. Out of the corner of my eye, I see Dax. He's still there, just watching me. "If you don't tell me why you're here, I'm going to call security."

"We don't have security."

Darn it. He's right. "I'll kick you out myself, then."

"I'd kind of like to see you try."

Given how successful I was at getting him to move from my desk, I'm thinking my odds wouldn't be all that great. *But you'd get to touch his muscles again.*

Ugh, staaaaaaahp thinking about the muscles, Alexis! Even if he's built like a Greek god, he's a terrible and annoying human being who you cannot wait to be rid of.

"RB?"

"What?" My face snaps back to his. He's wearing an unreadable expression—maybe slightly amused? Did he say something? My armpits start to itch.

He shakes his head then gets up and closes the door before returning to his seat. "I think we should concoct a backstory." A pause. "You know, for tomorrow night."

And there it is. My throat suddenly dry, I reach for my Hydro Flask and take a sip. Also dry. Argh. "Why do we need a backstory? Aren't I just there as proof that you have a fiancée?"

"Well, yeah, but I get the feeling that Fred and Tom —the guys who own the company and will be interviewing me tomorrow—will want to know our story. How we met, how we fell in love, how I asked you to marry me. That kind of stuff."

"Oh." That does make sense. Why else would they really want me along?

"Their wives are going to be there too," he continues. Right. I feel like maybe he mentioned that before. "Janet is Fred's wife, Cecilia is Tom's."

Reluctantly, I reach for a pen and notepad, and start writing down this information. "Okay, what else?"

He fills me in on the history of Bennett Toys. They've just got one location in Los Angeles and have been in business for fifty years. Fred and Tom Bennett are brothers and their dad started the business, passed it down to them. They make a variety of wooden, old-school toys that are still popular with kids today, and they're looking to expand their distribution, albeit slowly. Thus, the marketing director position they're looking to fill. It really does sound like a good, solid company, and the fact they want to hire people they can be friends with—that have the same familial values—actually makes sense.

There's a giddiness in Dax's voice as he describes all of this, an edge of something I haven't really heard from him before. I glance up mid-note to watch him as he tells me about Fred and Tom, what nice guys they are, how he would love to travel, to see more of the world because he's really only lived in California his whole life. I want to ask why, but I also feel strangely drawn to this version of him.

There's no mask, no pretense. I can tell he means what he's saying.

Something tightens in my gut. What am I thinking? Guys like Dax, they make it their mission to be fake in every way. I can't start to fall for his charms now. I'd be no better than anyone else who eats out of his palm in this office.

Clearing my throat, I press the pen to paper again. "Okay, so what about this backstory you think we need? Have you already come up with something?"

He places his hands behind his head and leans back in his chair, the splashes of color on my wall a perfect complement to the yellow button-down he's paired with jeans. "We should keep it as close to the truth as possible."

Nibbling the inside of my cheek, I nod. "So we met here at work."

"And you couldn't keep your eyes off of me."

I snort. "What version of the truth are you working with?"

"All right, all right. So you didn't like me at first—"

"Loathed you."

"Loathed me, right." He chuckles, like he doesn't believe what I'm saying. He should believe it, though. It's the truth. There's nothing about him I like. Not his stupid (albeit handsome) face, not the way his lips quirk up in the corner, and definitely not the way his eyes glint when he's telling a joke.

I grip my pen so tight, my fingers burn with tingles. "So how did we go from being enemies to—"

"Lovers?"

Oh my stars, now it's my insides that are aflame, and not just because of what he said, but the sensuous and teasing way in which he said it. Refusing to look at him, I cough and stare at my notes. "I was going to say engaged."

"Ah, right. That too."

Silence suspends between us, so taut I feel every crackle and my nerves are buzzing all over. I glance up to find those gold-flecked green eyes fixed on me, the most intense look on his face.

Finally, he speaks. "One day, out of the blue, I realized that you have the most vivacious brown eyes that spark and sizzle when you're angry, and I was powerless to resist their siren's call." Dax stands and walks around my desk toward me. My fingertips are now numb. "I held it in for days, weeks, but at long last, I simply had to tell you how you make me feel. How you make every moment more fun, how you challenge me, how you bring color into my life when I thought it was all drained out."

My heart is screaming its warnings at me. *We're under attack! Forcefields up. May day!* But I can't move, can't speak. Can only press my pen harder into the paper, needlessly spilling ink onto the pad, while he comes closer.

Then he's there, sitting on the edge of the desk right beside me, leaning into my airspace until he's close enough to hear my thumping pulse. Dax lingers, staying, his eyes fully engaged with mine, his face—his lips —just inches away.

I don't believe his words, not for a second. But then what is this hold he has over me, giving me the urge to grab his shirt and pull him in for a kiss? I know better. I do. But I can't help but wonder … what would he taste like?

Gah. "And what did I say when you, um, said all this?" Whose voice is that, all husky and breathy at the same time? It's some imposter Alexis, inhabiting my body and forcing me to act and speak like someone else. That's more plausible than me actually sounding like I'm almost flirting back.

A smile flickers across his lips and he reaches for my hand, threads our fingers together, our palms warm against one another. "You, of course, said you felt the same way. That you'd only been using hatred as a guise to resist the pull I had on you, but you couldn't hold back anymore. Then I kissed you and the rest, well, is history." He sits up abruptly, drops my hand, and retreats to his chair, a satisfied smirk on his face. "How was that? Pretty convincing, huh?"

I blink. *How was that?* That was … oh, this man! Ugh,

I knew it was all part of his scheme, an act. He's good—I'll give him that. A master manipulator of emotions. No wonder he's great at marketing.

Whatever I do, I cannot let him see he's rattled me. Cannot show that I am currently flexing my hand under the desk in an attempt to free it from his now phantom touch. Cannot reveal that I was taken in, even just a little —like an idiot—by his little performance.

"It'll do, I guess." I'm proud of myself for saying this without even a hint of a waver in my voice. "Oh, and what's the dress code for tomorrow, by the way?"

He studies me for a minute, seemingly searching for something in my gaze. A weakness, no doubt. But baby, this fortress has had years of experience with shutting down any inkling of emotions when it comes to guys, and it's certainly not breaking down for the likes of fakest-of-the-fake Dax Nyhart.

"Casual," he says, his head tilting. "The dress code is casual."

Good. I won't even have to dress up, and I survived holding his hand. That means I can do this thing tomorrow. For one evening, I can pretend to actually like, even love, him.

And then, hopefully, he will be out of my life forever.

five

. . .

CASUAL IS RIGHT.

So casual, I almost laugh the next evening when I walk up to the pizza joint where Bennett Toys is conducting Dax's second interview. A quick peek inside shows long picnic tables crammed together with booths next to a wall of arcade games. There seems to be a patio on one side with TVs broadcasting tonight's baseball game. As a couple exits, I can tell it's a bit on the loud side, rock music layered with laughter and kids' excited shouts.

Though the sky has darkened, the old-fashioned black streetlights make it easy to see Dax jogging up the sidewalk toward me. "Hey." He insisted on driving me over after work, but I was equally insistent that I could drive myself, and obviously I beat him here. Even though he told me the dress code was casual, he's changed from the polo and jeans he was wearing earlier into a collared shirt, dark jeans, and brown leather jacket. Still casual, but dressier too. I, on the other hand, am still wearing my clothes from today. If he doesn't like my skinny jeans, plain turquoise T-shirt, and purple Keds, tough.

"Hey," I say in reply.

When he reaches me, he cranes his neck around me, shifts from one foot to the other. "You ready for this?"

He's nervous. Honestly, I can't blame him. I hate interviews, and this seems like a job he really wants. What doesn't make sense is the hollowed out feeling in the pit of *my* stomach. Why am I nervous too? It can't be a sympathetic thing—I don't care how he feels.

I don't.

But maybe it's just the weirdness of the whole situation. I mean, this is literally the first time other than the annual holiday work party that I've seen him outside of the office. And that didn't count because it was still work related.

This *is* … but also isn't.

What am I doing here? "This is a terrible idea, Dax."

He blinks. "You're backing out on me?"

"No." I bite my lip. "I'm just letting you know that I don't think this is going to go well."

"Thanks for that vote of confidence." The sidewalk is getting more crowded as the evening wears on, and I really hope that Fred and Tom—and their wives—don't choose this moment to walk up. "That's something I admire about you, Alexis. You always tell it like it is. Even when people don't want to hear it."

Is he being sarcastic? I can't tell, but guess it doesn't matter. I shrug. "Sorry not sorry."

"Well, in any case, we'd better get inside." He starts for the door, then pauses and digs into his pocket. "Oh. I almost forgot." His hand emerges and he presents an object to me, palm up. "This is for you."

I freeze. "Is that … Lilith's engagement ring?" It's gorgeous, and kind of vintage, with two blue roses—made of sapphires and diamonds—twining together. But the idea of wearing another woman's ring, even for just a few hours, doesn't sit well with me.

He laughs, but there's something stilted in it. "No. She called *that* her consolation prize and sold it after the engagement ended. At least, I assume she did." A pause, and he shakes his head. "This one's a fake. But it kind of looked like something you might wear."

I ignore the warmth creeping into my middle at that statement. "Okay." Holding out my left hand, I pray Dax doesn't notice its slight tremor as he slips the ring on my fourth finger.

After examining it for a moment, he nods. "Let's do this." He reaches for my hand and I just stare at it. Dax sighs. "Come on, Alexis. I won't bite."

"You sure about that?"

He laughs. "You really need to loosen up or no one is going to believe you actually like me."

"Well, I don't." I cross my arms over my chest. "And I'm not a good actor like some people I know."

"All right, close your eyes."

"What?" I narrow my eyes at him. "Why?"

"You really aren't very trusting, are you?"

Not of men in general, and definitely not of him. But the quicker I comply, the quicker we can go in there and get this night over with. "Fine." I do as he asks, and the world goes dark.

"Okay, now I want you to envision the office as quiet, without me in it, pestering you by being my suave and handsome self."

It's difficult to roll your eyes while they're closed, but I manage to do it. I think. "Your annoying self, you mean."

"Whatever you want to tell yourself. Either way, picture a Dax-free office."

Ah. Peace. A shot at the best accounts, at getting the bonuses that come with them, at paying off my mortgage so I can live a quiet life without new housemates. The thought brings a genuine smile to my face.

"I'm wounded, RB."

My grin grows wider, this time a teasing taunt.

"Wow. Okay, then."

I open my eyes to find him shaking his head, a slight smile on his lips. "Let's go, RB."

"Hold up," I say. "No more of that."

"What?"

"Rainbow Brite. RB. It's a ridiculous nickname, and if I'm doing you this favor, I'm demanding you quit calling me that. At least for tonight."

"We have to be convincing." He steps closer. "And fiancés usually have pet names for each other."

"Like Daxy?" That's what Lilith called him the one time I met her. Stupidest nickname ever, if you ask me. And the way she drawled it out in a singsong voice. Gag me.

He flinches, then recovers. "Yeah, like that. Except …

maybe not that one in particular?"

Aw, shoot, I'm feeling that emotion again. What's it called? Oh yeah. Guilt. I really should be nicer about Lilith. I mean, Dax *was* engaged to her and it sounds like maybe she left him for a different kind of life. He probably is a little sensitive about it.

"Fine," I concede. "You can call me something respectable. Like darling or dear." I grimace, because the thought of Dax calling me any sort of term of endearment is cringe-inducing. But I can take one for the team. For two hours. Max.

"Sure." An evil sort of chuckle rolls from Dax's throat. "I'll have to try out a few *respectable* nicknames to see what sticks. Now come on." And before I can protest, he has the door open. "Ladies first."

I breeze past him and the air from inside blows against my hair, which is in its customary braid. He comes up beside me and then waves at someone across the room. "There they are." Dax places a hand on the small of my back and steers me toward two couples sitting at a large round booth in the back corner.

His fingers burn through the fabric of my shirt. "Dax," I whisper out of the side of my mouth.

"What?" he hisses back.

"If your hand moves south of the equator, that's definitely finger-chop-worthy."

His deep chuckle brings goosebumps to my forearms. "Noted."

Before I can even take another breath, we are at the table and doing this thing. All four of the people scooch out of the booth, and Dax introduces me to Fred and

Tom, two men in their fifties with round bellies and jovial smiles, who in turn introduce us to Janet and Cecilia. Their wives—both heavy chested with manicures, silky patterned sleeveless shirts that probably cost more than my car, and matching coiffed shoulder-length hair (Janet's is blondish gray, while Cecilia's is black to complement her tawny skin)—embrace first Dax and then me warmly, and Cecilia kisses both of my cheeks before retaking her seat.

Dax gestures that I should sit first, so I scoot in next to Janet, who smells like lavender and vanilla. Then he joins me, and because of how tight the booth is, his shoulder presses up against mine. My eyes flick upward at him, but he's hyper focused on the others at our table.

Tom smiles at us both. "It's such a pleasure to meet you, Alexis."

"You too, sir."

"Aw, none of that, now." He waves his hand in the air, and the other three titter. "We don't stand on formality here. In fact"—he signals a server—"I'm going to order a few pitchers of beer if that's all right with you?"

"You are my people!" The enthusiastic words pop out before I can think to hold them in. I don't want them all to think Dax's fiancée is a lush or reflect poorly on him before this interview has even started. "I mean, I hate formality too."

Our server, a red-headed teenage girl, arrives with water for everyone. In addition to the beer, Tom takes the liberty of ordering salads, bread sticks, and pizzas for the whole table.

Once the server is gone, Cecilia reaches across the table and pats my hand. "I'm sure you've had a long week, but it's time to relax now, dear."

My eyebrows dart northward. "I'm relaxed."

Dax laughs under his breath beside me and I pinch the side of his leg. He gets revenge by grabbing my fingers and moving our joined hands to the top of the table for all to see.

The jerk.

I blow out a breath and return my attention to Cecilia, whose astute gaze is still fixed on me.

"You're among friends, Alexis."

"Of course. But, this is also an interview, right?"

"Oh, she's straightforward. Honest. I like this one, Dax," Fred says.

"I do too." Dax squeezes my hand, looks down at me with eyes filled with loving. Fake loving. And a spark of something else. Maybe irony? His lips twitch. "You know how much, right, Nutter Butter?"

Oh, he didn't. Respectable nicknames, my rear. I grit my teeth, force a smile. Dig my fingernails into his palm. "Of course." I nearly call him Daxy just to get even, but I don't want to throw him off so much that he tanks this interview. It needs to go well.

"Well," Cecilia continues, drawing my attention to her once again. "Personally, I could tell from the second you walked in that you were a kindred spirit."

What does that even mean? "Um, thank you." With my free hand, I grab my water and take a sip.

Fred and Tom erupt into laughter, and Tom squeezes his wife's shoulder. "If Cecilia declares it, we believe it."

Janet nods. "It's true. She's a very spiritual person. Can sense things in others. It's uncanny, really." She wrinkles her nose, her eyes sparkling. "She knew that Fred and I would get married before we even did. At the time, I was just the company receptionist, saving up money to get out of dodge since I grew up here. I dreamed of bigger and better things."

"Then she met me. I'm definitely bigger." Fred pats his round stomach. "Not so sure I'm better, but she puts up with me." He winks at her, and all of them laugh again.

"How long have you all been married?" Dax asks.

"Not long enough." Janet snuggles against Fred's chest, which puffs up at her admiration. "Thirty-three years this December."

"And thirty-seven for us last month," Tom chimes in. He pushes a finger against one side of his bulbous nose. "Look, sweetie, I remembered."

"I'm so proud of you."

Okay, okay, these people are … kind of cute. And they seem genuine. This is something I've not really seen. Marriages that last this long. I mean, I know it happens, but I've always assumed that those who have stuck out so many decades of marriage are either miserable or just don't spend much time together.

But the Bennetts don't seem miserable. In fact, both couples seem very much in love, if the way they're holding hands and leaning into each other is any indication.

The server brings us our beer and bread, lets us know the pizzas will be out in about twenty minutes.

"How about you, Dax, Alexis?" Janet lifts a piece of cheesy garlic bread off the plate, its melted topping stretching thin as she separates it from the rest. "How long have you been together?"

"Oh." I smile tight. "You don't want to hear about that. Why don't we talk about Dax and all of his qualifications for this job?" That's why we're here, right? *Please, let's just get on with this.* This dwelling on love and marriage is all a bit … disconcerting. Depressing.

Livin' on a Prayer bursts through the speakers overhead, and I suddenly feel seen by the cosmic forces.

Tom wags his finger at me. "We know all of that already. Dax is fully qualified. What we want to see is how he—how both of you—fit in with us. He probably told you this, but family is our most important priority."

Dax squeezes my fingers. "I told her, but Schnookums here had a hard time believing it. She's got herself so tied up in knots over this because she wants it so badly for the both of us. Isn't that right, Biscuit?"

Schnookums? And Biscuit? Like the dog from that children's book series?

That's it. Two can play this game. "Oh, but Dax is always such a tease. I never quite know when he's pulling my leg. Isn't that right, Booger Bear?"

He takes a quick drink, only half concealing his snort. "It sure is, Snap Pea."

I open my mouth to retort when Cecilia laughs. "You two are so playful and fun." She places her chin on her hands, which are propped up by her elbows on the table. "I love it. Now, we are getting your story out of you sooner or later, but first, Alexis, why don't you tell us the thing you love most about Dax? I'd love to see him through your eyes."

"I know there are so many traits you admire." Dax grins down at me. "Take your time, Lady-Loves-A-Lot."

I have the sudden urge to cram a fork down his throat, but instead I press my lips together and tap my chin with my free hand—my other's still being held prisoner in Dax's. "I love …"

His expectant eyes spark at me, his lips tilt. He thinks he's got me.

And I know just the thing.

"His mouth."

"Ooo, I'll bet," Janet snickers as Fred tops off her beer.

Dax's teeth flash white in the room that's grown dimmer as the sun has fully disappeared outside. "I *am* a good kisser, aren't I?"

"Oh, I guess, Hunk-a-Lunk." I wink. "But your mouth is also just so … useful."

"Useful?" His eyebrows pitch together like pick-up sticks, and I can't tell where one ends and the other begins.

"Mm hmm." I casually take a sip of beer, sigh with pleasure.

The gang looks at one another, then back at me. "Care to elaborate, Alexis?" Tom asks, amusement in his tone.

"Oh, right." I laugh, and it's light and airy like I don't have a care in the world. Meanwhile, Dax is squeezing the life outta my hand. "Well, at a recent company party, we had a tater tot eating contest. I know, sexy, right? And this guy"—I thumb him in the chest … the ultra-hard chest—"crammed twenty-one into that lovely mouth of his, leading our team to victory. Impressive, right?"

I go on drinking my beer while the rest of the table seems to wait for the punchline. Dax shifts in his seat.

Oh, crud. Maybe I sounded a bit too sarcastic for their liking. They did ask me an earnest question after all, and were probably looking for a genuine answer. I swallow, turn my focus back to him. "But in all seriousness"—the table seems to breathe a sigh of relief that I was just joking—"he, um, has a way with words. Of making everyone feel known and cherished."

I nearly gag on the words coming from my mouth, because saying nice things about Dax is at the top of the list of things I never plan to do—right there alongside going to prison and forgiving Corbin for cheating on me.

But honestly, it's the truth. There *is* something about Dax that people love, and even if I don't personally feel that way about him, maybe I've been somehow blind, prejudiced against him because of my past. Or maybe he really is just nothing but a charmer. And there's the rub. I really don't know which it is.

At my words, though, Dax stiffens. His hold on my hand loosens. His Adam's apple bobs. Not exactly the reaction I thought I'd get from saying something kind.

"And …?" Janet prods.

Knowing what she wants to hear, I playfully roll my eyes. "And fine. His kissing isn't terrible."

The table erupts into cheers, and Dax releases a

breath. The spell is broken. He raises his glass. "Hear, hear."

At just that moment, the pizzas arrive and while the others are busy getting everything situated on the table, Dax leans closer. *"Isn't terrible,* huh? What a glowing recommendation."

"I've gotta speak as I find."

"We could really sell this thing and you could find out for yourself one way or the other. For our cover story's sake, of course."

I can't help but shiver at the tease in his voice, the suggestion he's just made. But I don't let on that he's got me wondering if what I said isn't actually the truth …

Instead, I smile and speak through my teeth. "You can stick that idea where the sun don't shine, Casanova."

With his chuckle in my ear, we all grab slices of pizza and the conversation flows freely. Dax seems totally comfortable with the Bennetts, but then again, he seems comfortable with most people. The odd thing? I find myself relaxing with them too, laughing for real. That only ever happens with my friends.

What is this magic that they've cast on me? I'm almost sad that I'll never see them again.

By the end of the night, Janet is fairly wasted, but she's an adorable older-lady drunk who keeps stroking her husband's shirt and telling him she wants to take him home for some "canoodling." Cecilia yawns and says it's past her bedtime. Tom pays and we all saunter out, Dax and I loaded up with the leftovers.

I'm immediately enveloped by another couple of

hugs, made warmer by the few hours we just spent together, and when Cecilia leans in, she whispers softly in my ear. "You and Dax sure do have something special. And if I have any say—which, let's be honest, I do—Dax will be our new marketing director."

The thought should send a pulse of joy through me. My goal, to be rid of Dax Nyhart, is coming to fruition.

But something else skips a rock against my heart instead. These people are lovely, and I've just spent the evening lying to them. What's worst, I find myself almost wishing that the pretense could go on even more.

Not because I like Dax or anything. No. Ick. I'm thankful my hands are currently occupied holding the pizza box so I don't have to hold his anymore. Because that would be ... despicable. Unfathomable. Unbearable.

But genuine people like the Bennetts are few and far between in this world, and I wouldn't mind having dinner with them again. Too bad that's not in the cards. Because even if Dax gets the job, I won't be at future dinners.

The Bennetts wave goodbye and walk off in the opposite direction. Dax turns to me. "Good job in there, RB."

"Oh, we're back to that, are we?"

"I could call you Lovey-Dovey if you prefer."

"Or, you know, Alexis."

He scrunches his nose, shakes his head. "Nah, I don't think Alexis suits you."

"Ha ha." We start walking toward our cars. "Seems like it went well, though, don't you think?"

"I do."

We're quiet for the rest of the three-minute walk, dodging people on the street, which is in full weekend mode. Restaurants nearby are hopping, music is booming from a karaoke bar, and streetlamps from the beach parking lot down the way fling light at the sky.

Dax and I finally reach the lot where we both parked. I stop beside my car and put the pizza box on top, then dig in my purse for my keys. "I guess let me know when you hear something."

He leans against my driver's-side door. "Bet you can't wait to be rid of me." There's almost something searching in this tone.

"You know it." I clear my throat, stare at him, but he just stays there, looking back at me. What does he want me to say? My end of the bargain is over. "So remember. If you do get the job …"

"I'll tell Nate you deserve all of my accounts. Yep."

"And you're still going to let me choose the three I want, yeah?"

He nods. "Just text me which ones you want."

"Any three."

"That's what I agreed to, wasn't it?" He shoves his hands in his pockets and looks out across the parking lot, toward the beach a mile away. The moon hangs low on the horizon tonight, big and yellow and streaked with character.

I can't explain it, but Dax seems suddenly morose. Uneasy. I sense that he's tired, that his mask has slipped, and there's some part of me that wants to ask him what's wrong. But do I really want to know? What would be the point? I have no desire to be his friend. There's something about him that throws me off kilter.

I really and truly can't wait to be rid of him.

Really? Truly?

Yeah. That's what I said.

Now I'm talking to myself. Ugh. Yeah. I need to … go. "Um, can you move, please? My roommates will be sending out a search party for me soon." They won't, actually. Lauren and Shelby are out tonight with Evie and Kayla for our monthly girls' night. No one was happy when I canceled, but they understand I had a work commitment.

That's all they know. A work commitment. And they will never know more than that, if I have anything to say about it. The teasing would never end.

"Right." Dax steps aside, and I press my key fob, open my door. "Thanks again for doing this, Alexis. You were great in there. A better actor than you thought." Again with the searching something in his voice.

Does he … he has to know nothing I said in there was true, right? That, even though it was admittedly kind of nice to hold his hand all night, to meet new people who were sweet and generous, this thing between us … it was all fake.

It didn't mean anything.

"Yeah." I twist the ring off my finger and shove it into his hand before ducking into my car and reaching for the pizza. "I guess I am."

After he gives me the box, I close the door, start up the car, and drive home where I may or may not proceed to eat all of the leftovers in one sitting.

six

. . .

I CAN ONLY ASSUME Dax didn't get the job.

It's been ten days since our fake date, and I feel certain Tom and Fred would have offered someone the job by now. If Dax didn't get it, the married guy with three kids must have. So looks like I'm stuck with Dax after all. It hasn't been so bad, since he's mostly avoided me except for our very brief interactions regarding work stuff.

And he's been true to his word about the accounts. I asked for Aretha's account and two others I was positive he wouldn't give me, but he turned them over without question. The bonus money was deposited into my account on Friday, just a week after our meeting with the Bennetts. I'm that much closer to gaining financial independence, being debt free. Not needing to find new roommates when mine move out. (Which is a good thing, because *next* Halloween, I'll be left in peace instead of being forced to dress up like Black Widow and hand out candy with Cinderella Shelby and Boy-Band-Groupie Lauren. But I digress.)

Not that all of this stopped Nate from giving Dax the newest client—another big one. His reason? Since I've freed up some of Dax's time, he needs to refill his roster. Like I buy that for a second. It doesn't matter how much I "prove" myself. As long as Dax is here, he's going to continue to get the best accounts. And I'm powerless to stop it. That's one reason I was really hoping to hear he'd landed the job at Bennett Toys.

The other reason? My dreams.

Ever since our dinner with the Bennetts, it's like my mind has been betraying me while I've been asleep. Because it's been imagining things. Impossible things. Things I don't want. Can't want.

Remembering the feel of his hand in mine, the subtle brush of his thumb against my skin. Reliving the warmth of his breath on the tip of my earlobe as he leaned forward to whisper something snarky during dinner. Dreaming of putting his kissing prowess to the test.

Like I said. Impossible—and entirely unwanted.

I really hoped he'd be getting the job, if only so he'd be out of San Diego for good and the ridiculous dreams would stop attacking my subconscious.

Ugh. Enough dwelling on *that*. "It is what it is," I whisper to myself. My shoulders ache as I push back from my office chair, swiveling my stiff neck this way and that. How long have I been sitting here, working on a fresh design for Longenecker Homes' new line of cleaning products? A quick glance at the clock on my laptop says five hours straight. Oof. Time to go home. It's been a Monday, that's for sure.

As I'm packing up my bag, someone knocks on my door. It's Dax. "Hey. Can we talk?"

"Just packing up to leave, but yeah, come in." I unzip my bag, the sound shooting through the room, filling the silence. Then I start to load in my phone, my mango ChapStick, my water bottle.

He steps inside, glances down the hallway, and closes the door behind him. His hair is loosened from the hold of the gel he uses. It's his end-of-the-day, gonna-go-lounge-on-the-couch look, and something about it sends heat through my stomach. "On Friday, I got a call from Fred."

My hands freeze. "Yeah?"

"Yeah."

"And?" I set my purse aside. "Did you get the job?"

"Not exactly." He smiles, but it's grim. Unsettling.

But honest.

That makes me sit up straighter. My hands need something to do, so I resume zipping my bag. Then unzipping it. Rezipping it. "Out with it, Nyhart."

"I liked it better when you called me Booger Bear. Maybe BB for short."

"So RB and BB?"

He grins. "Has a ring to it, don't you think?"

I can't help it. I laugh. "Okay, BB. So? What does 'not exactly' mean?"

The grin falls from his lips. In fact, his whole countenance slumps and he reaches up to scratch behind his ear. (And I absolutely do NOT notice the stretch and formation of his bicep at this movement. No, I do not.)

"Well," he begins. He's the tortoise and I'm the hare and I want to shake him to go faster, go faster. "They still can't decide between the other guy—Landon—and me."

"Landon. Ugh. What kind of name is that?"

"Right?" Dax sits in the chair, puts his head in his hand, takes a deep breath, then looks up at me again. What in the world? "So, they've come up with a way to decide. It's crazy. So not traditional. But then again …"

"Neither are they."

"Yeah." The way he looks at me, it's like his puppy died or something.

"Well, maybe … maybe it's just not meant to be." Who *am* I, giving Dax Nyhart a pep talk? And they say people can't evolve. "There are other jobs."

"Yeah, but this one just feels so right, Alexis. You met them. They feel like family."

"Dax, I hate to be so on the nose about this, but you literally work with family. Why do you need a new job so badly?"

"That's the *problem* with this job." He stands again, paces. I'm sensing a trend with him. "My uncle is great, but he's taken care of me, of my family, for too long. It's time for me to man up, be on my own. And even if it means I have to move away from my … family … at least this way I can …" He trails off.

I study him, take full notice of the way he's running his hands through his hair, tugging at the bottom of his shirt. He's not happy-go-lucky-flirtatious Dax. He's something altogether different.

He's honest Dax. Authentic Dax.

And he's never been more attractive.

Oh no. This can't be happening. Where is the wall I've spent years erecting around my heart? *Don't fail me now, you stupid fortress! There cannot be a hole when I need you most. Get. It. Together.*

He continues. "The job comes with a raise, one I'd never get here—Nate just doesn't have the resources to pay me as much as this one would. And I need the money."

I'm going to regret asking this. I am. I shouldn't care about Dax, about his life, his reasons. And yet ... "Why do you need the money?"

"I just do, okay?"

I hold up my hands. That's what I get for trying to show an interest in someone else's life. Serves me right. "Okay, okay." A pause hangs in the air like a misplaced semi-colon. "So what's this magical plan Fred and Tom have concocted to decide between you and Landon?"

He bites the corner of his lip and I can't help but find it kind of sexy. (Maybe I wasn't lying when I said I appreciated Dax's mouth. Oof.) "More time with each of the candidates."

Ah. This is why he's so down—he thinks I'll say no to another dinner. "Give me three more clients and I'll go out to dinner with you again."

He frowns, and dang, looks fairly miserable. More like a beloved grandma died, not a puppy. Okay, maybe not that extreme, but still. Dude looks utterly dejected.

"Kidding. I'll do it for one client." I can't go giving it to him for free. I've got a reputation to uphold.

But he just shakes his head. "A cruise."

"What?"

"They want to take us on a cruise."

My heart bursts in my chest—and not a yay-I'm-happy kind of bursting. More like a the-world-is-exploding-and-so-am-I kind. "A cruise."

"Yeah."

"Like … a harbor cruise?" Those can last hours. Surely he can't mean—

"Like, a nine-day cruise. To the Caribbean. Just before Thanksgiving."

Oh, wait. "You're not serious, right?" I snort, and then utterly delicious giggles find me, the kind that offer relief to the pang I'd been feeling inside. "That's a good one, though. What an idea. Conducting a long-range interview by inviting candidates on cruises. They're not *that* crazy."

I expect to see Dax's usual grin, hear a "gotcha!" But that doesn't happen. Instead, his shoulders sink and his head with it. "It's not a joke."

My laughter dies abruptly in my throat. "That's unreal."

He shrugs. "Maybe, but they're filthy rich and want people who are committed enough to put their lives on hold and take a vacation with them. They said they won't decide until after the trip. That both Landon and I are invited—us and our significant others." He cocks his head. "You could think of it as a fully-paid vacation?"

The question at the end of the sentence does not

compute. I process what he said. *Us and our significant others.*

"Hold up." I stand, and now I'm the one pacing. "You want me to drop all of my work here and go on this cruise with you? Pretend for a whole week and a half to be engaged to you? I have a life, you know."

"Do you? A life outside of work?"

"Yes." I mean, sort of, if you count talking to my sister weekly and going out with my friends when they're not busy with their husbands and fiancés.

"Come on, Alexis. You never take vacation and I know you have PTO stored up. Nate values work-life balance. He'd say yes to the last-minute time off for both of us. You know he would."

He would. But that's not the point. Oh, my head aches. I push a hand against my temple and rub, shutting my eyes. "You said something about Thanksgiving. My sister is coming to visit. The timing … it just doesn't work for me."

"We'd fly out the twelfth—the cruise leaves the thirteenth but we have to give ourselves time to fly across the country and spend the night in Fort Lauderdale. Then we'd get back on the twenty-first, which is three days before Thanksgiving."

Shoot. Kennedy isn't planning to come until the twenty-third. But still. This is Monday. The twelfth is Saturday. Five days from now. My eyes open and I spear him with a look. "I only agreed to one dinner, Dax. One dinner. I didn't sign up for *this*."

It'd be too much. Impossible. Not only the timing,

but spending so much time with Dax. My dreams would have a freaking field day with that.

"I know you didn't." He stands again, kicks at the carpet. "I knew it was a long shot. But just … well, look. I don't think I'll get the job if I don't go. Or if I go and you don't."

I get what he's not saying. If I don't go, he won't get the job—and then things will just go on as they have before. Maybe Nate respects me a bit more now that I'm handling some bigger clients, but I'll always be competing with Dax. Do I care as much about that if I'm paying off my mortgage, though? Still. If he's here, I might not be able to pay it off by the time I'd need new roommates. But if I can get all of those lovely accounts … all of those bonuses … well, it'll be a happy Thanksgiving and Merry Christmas to me.

And what about after that? I want to put Kennedy through school. At least give her the option, because I really don't think her grandma will turn over her trust fund unless she does. But there's no way my base salary would cover that.

I want to say no. I really, really do. It's a matter of survival. I mean, honestly, one dinner with Dax has me dreaming crazy things—what will ten days together do?

Ugh. I have no idea what to say. And there's no one to ask objectively for their opinion either. If I ask Kennedy, I know what she'll say, can just picture it. "*A free vacation with a hot guy? And the possibility of getting all his clients if he lands the job? What's there to decide?*"

I mean, maybe she has a point. (Or would have a point, if I bothered to ask her.) A vacation could be nice.

And sure, Dax would be there, and we'd have to pretend to be engaged, but it would continue to be a business transaction. One that would come with the perk of a tan and some free time to read on the cruise ship deck.

I can handle that, right?

"I can't believe I'm about to say this."

At my words, his head pops up.

"I'll do it." He opens his mouth to respond, but I hold up a hand. "But I have stipulations."

"I wouldn't expect any less. Let's hear them."

"Well, the first and most obvious? And I don't care how it looks. You can tell people we are traditional. Don't care. But we will not, under any circumstances, share a room."

"Anything else?"

I arch an eyebrow. "How much time do you have?"

seven

· · ·

THE DOORBELL RINGS JUST as I'm zipping up my suitcase in my room. My eyes flit to the clock on my bright-pink bedside table. Why is Dax thirty minutes early?

I mean, I'm ready. Couldn't sleep last night—thought so many times about canceling, claiming to be sick, but ultimately, my reasons for going haven't changed. And when I told Kennedy about it, she pretty much said what I figured she would, confirming that I made the right decision. She also said, *"I'm proud of you, sis. Doing something fun for once."*

Sure. Fun. Spending ten days with the coworker I can't stand and pretending to be in love with him.

Yay.

Okay, fine, maybe he's not AS BAD as I thought, but he's still a guy. And a man plus my heart does not equal anything but a terrible idea.

"Business, Alexis," I mutter. "Just business."

The doorbell rings again. I'm surprised Shelby hasn't answered it yet, but maybe she left with Eric already to do cake testing this morning on their day off. Lauren, to my knowledge, is at work. Which is good. I didn't want any of them to meet Dax anyway.

Not that they know I'm going with him. They think I am going with Kennedy. Well, they might have assumed that and I might have let them. So sue me. When Dax insisted on coming to get me, I said I'd find my own way to the airport but then all of my friends were busy. And because I wasn't willing to pay to park at the airport for so long, I finally relented.

I leave behind my suitcase and head to the front door, opening it before I have a chance to look through the peephole.

And there stand Kayla and Evie. Kayla has a zippered duffel and steps forward. "Hey, Alexis! We totally thought you'd be gone by now." She steps inside, right past me. "I just have some maternity clothes Shelby's sister-in-law let me borrow. Now that I'm as big as a house, they don't fit anymore, so I'm returning them to her. Be right back." And she leaves Evie and me standing there.

My forehead scrunches. "What are you doing here? I thought you guys weren't available to take me to the airport."

Evie hugs her stomach, her hand absently massaging the bottom of it, right near her hip. "Can I come in?"

"Oh yeah, sure." I step aside and she joins me, peeking down the hallway. "What's going on, Evie?"

"Well." She worries her bottom lip as she glances

around our living room. "Man. So many memories in this house." Her eyes get all teary. "Sorry. Pregnancy hormones. I thought I was past all of that craziness with the first trimester, but the third is something else. I'm just so … tired."

"Okay." I steer her toward the couch and sit her down. "Hang on." After I retrieve a water from the fridge, I walk it back to her and make her prop her feet up on the coffee table. "Here." I shove the bottle into her hands.

She doesn't twist the lid, just lays her head back against the cushions. "Thanks. Sorry again for barging in here."

She didn't really apologize for barging in in the first place, but since she brought it up again … "I really don't mind, except I'm curious why you guys told me you were busy but are here now."

"I told Kayla this was a bad idea."

"What?" Kayla's been gone an awfully long time, now that I think of it. I hear a door close down the hallway, but Kayla doesn't emerge at first. I turn my eyes to Evie, spear her with a look.

As usual, my friend crumples under the pressure. A hand goes over her eyes. "We made it up. We're all here because we know you're actually going on this cruise with Dax and we want to meet him." Her words come out so quickly it takes me a few long seconds to process them.

By the time I do, Shelby, Lauren, and Kayla poke their heads into the living room.

"Way to be, Evie the Unbreakable." Kayla shakes her

head, looks between Shelby and Lauren. "I thought Shelby would be the weakest link, but looks like it was always going to be Evie."

"You guys know I can't keep a secret!" Evie wails.

"Excuse me," I say, waving my hand. "Hi there. Um, what the heck, you guys?" How do they know … "Kennedy told you, didn't she?"

"Shelby called her to ask about your favorite treat so she could sneak some into your bag, but then Kennedy told us the truth." Evie bites her lip.

While Kayla waltzes in and plops unceremoniously into the patchwork chair, Shelby steps gingerly into the room and lowers herself on the other side of me. "I'm sorry, Alexis. We should have told you. Are you mad?"

"What she means is, *you* should have told us." Lauren leans against the wall next to the TV. "Why didn't you?"

"Because I knew you guys would do this. Make it a bigger deal than it is."

"Um, pretending to be engaged to your 'mortal enemy' kind of *is* a big deal." Kayla tilts her head. "Which begs the question … is he still your mortal enemy, or is there more going on?"

"I'm not talking about this with you guys." I grab a throw pillow and bury my face in it. "You are the literal worst."

"Alexis," Evie says in her gentle way. She rubs my back. I want to shrug off her hand, but I know that would hurt her feelings.

The thing is, there is a reason I didn't tell my friends. It's the same reason I've never told them about my dad.

About Corbin. About anything that really matters, honestly.

"Talk to us." That from Shelby.

I pull my face away from the soft pillow, breathe the free air again, and thoughts come tumbling out. "I'm just not used to telling people stuff, you know? For a lot of my life, I was alone. The girls at my boarding school hated me. My mom didn't want me around after my dad died. And even when Kennedy lived here, she was too young to really confide in. Like, fully confide, you know? Now we talk regularly, but I still think I hold a lot back."

If my friends are surprised about how much I've spoken in the last minute, they don't show it. In fact, all I see in each of their eyes is acceptance. Warmth.

Love.

My throat snags on a lump as I swallow.

"And why do you think that is?" Lauren asks.

"I'm the big sister. My job is to protect her, not to burden her with stuff."

"I get that." Lauren again. Having a younger sister who lives in New York, who she spent years not talking to, she really *does* get it. "But besides the fact I think you're underselling her, what about us? Why didn't you tell us?"

"Because." I stand, walk away toward the back door, swivel. "Because I knew exactly what you'd all say. Evie the romantic would tell me that she fell in love with her husband when they pretended to date. Lauren the encourager would tell me she loves me and supports me no matter what—which is nice, but wouldn't help me make any sort of decisions. Shelby the nurturer would tell me that people aren't always what they seem and maybe to give Dax a chance."

One by one, their jaws drop as the accuracy of my observations hits home. Funny how much I know them and how little they seem to know me.

Then again, that's on me, isn't it? I haven't *let them* see me. I've been so afraid they'd abandon me too that I've spent years hiding my heart away from them. But even now, when Evie and Kayla live elsewhere, they're here because I needed them—even if I never in a million years would have admitted it.

I'm not sure I even knew it.

"And what about me?" Kayla crosses her legs at the ankles, her eyes snapping in challenge. "What would I have said?"

"Well, that one's easy." Shelby laughs.

Evie joins in. "Totally."

"Yep," Lauren says.

Kayla looks around and lifts her eyebrows. "I'm sorry, what's so funny?"

My lips curve into a smile. "You'd say the same thing to me that you basically said to each of the others. Kayla the dating coach would tell me to just—"

"Grab that man and kiss him!" all four of us yell at the same time.

"Well." Kayla crosses her arms over her chest and harrumphs. "It's solid advice."

We all dissolve into laughter—even Kayla—so hard tears start coming fast and strong. Oh man. I needed this. I need them. Sobering, I travel back to Evie and sit again. "I know I don't say this often, but I love you guys."

Silence descends. Then Kayla—of course it's Kayla—speaks. "Often? I don't know that you've ever said it, Alexis."

Is that true? Am I so damaged that I could love my friends fiercely—so much I'd die for them—and have never told them? My mouth hangs open in indecision, and I stare at the rug. "Well, I do."

"Group hug!" Lauren squeals and vaults toward the couch, sitting squarely on Shelby, who oomphs with the extra weight on her lap.

Kayla hops up. "Preggo coming through!"

When she tries to sit on me, I hold up my hands, press them into her back. "Stop! I want to go on this cruise, not to the hospital because my back is broken."

"How rude!" But she's not actually offended. Instead, she sort of half sits, half lays across Shelby and me, and I'm afraid she's going to roll right off and onto the carpet.

Our joint laughter makes me feel twelve again—back before I knew the truth about my dad. My mom, dad, and I spent a whole night watching family home videos and eating popcorn, laughing at the silly memories. That's the last time I laughed like this.

And all because I opened myself up to them. Not even a lot. Just a little.

What if that could happen with a man?

Have I been wrong this whole time? Could opening my heart actually bring something other than bondage, than betrayal? Something other than dependence on someone bound to fail me?

Before I can contemplate this much-too-big-for-this-moment question, the doorbell rings again. There are squeals and hushed conversation as I extract myself from the group hug and make my way to the door. Before I answer, I turn to the group. "Behave."

And miraculously, all of my friends do. They shake Dax's hand, smile, and make pleasant conversation while I head to my bedroom for my suitcase and the backpack of essentials I'll need for tonight's hotel stay. Once I've brought my stuff to the front door, he smiles at me, and I feel it all the way to the bottom of my toes. He looks rather delicious in his white linen shirt and gray shorts. Behind him, Kayla gives me a thumbs-up and fans herself like she's about to faint.

I make cut-it-out eyes at her.

"Ready to go?" Dax asks.

"Yeah," I cough, smiling and praying he didn't catch my glance. "Of course." I say the words, but suddenly my heart isn't so sure. Only the encouraging smiles of my friends—and their bracing hugs—give me the courage to follow Dax out that door.

Of course, Kayla's whispered, "Remember my very solid advice!" does nothing to soothe and quiet my nerves. What have I gotten myself into?

But no. This is Dax. Annoying, charming-to-a-fault Dax, who is literally lying to get what he wants. And yes, I'm helping him so I get what I want. Which actually makes me just as bad. So who am I to really judge him?

"Just a business transaction," I say as I climb into the passenger side of the car.

"What's that?" Dax ducks inside.

"Nothing." I grip my phone in my lap. Maybe it's not too late to text my friends for an emergency extraction.

"Cool." Sliding on his shades, Dax starts up the car and reverses out of the driveway. "Feel free to choose the music. You're in control."

I relax at the reminder. Yes, I've got this. All these stupid emotions? I can totally tamp them down. I'm good at that. I'll simply remind them that, no matter how my knees betray me with their Jell-O-like qualities upon contemplating Dax's physical appearance, I in no uncertain terms am looking for a relationship.

Because the last one nearly did me in. Plus, Dax isn't looking to be serious with anyone either.

Yep, I'm in control. At least, I really, really hope so.

eight

. . .

WHY DID I think this kind of vacation could be nice?

Twelve hours in an airport or plane. Check. (The only amusing part? Seeing Dax squeezed between two large, burly men on the five-and-a-half-hour flight from California to Florida.)

An overnight stay in a hotel that had weekend construction going on in the room above mine. Check. (Thankfully, Dax and I had separate rooms, just like we will on the cruise ship.)

And now, I've climbed aboard a floating vessel that will be home to three thousand—three THOUSAND—people. Did I mention I hate crowds? No? Well, I do. And now I'm crammed aboard a crowd-infested ship watching the cruise ship pull farther and farther away from the dock in Fort Lauderdale. Land is becoming smaller, the ocean larger.

I cannot turn back. Can't escape.

Except to my room. That's the one haven. If things get too intense, I'll have a retreat from the noise.

From Dax.

Speaking of, I turn to find him standing beside me at the deck railing. His shoulders are relaxed, and between his cotton Tommy Bahama shirt, blue board shorts, and sunglasses, he looks ready-made for a Caribbean vacay. At least with it being November, the air isn't sticky with heat. "When did you say we can go to our rooms?"

Fred, Tom, and their wives—and Landon Meyer and his wife, Gloria, who we met briefly—all went off to their rooms an hour ago. The travel really did in Cecilia and Gloria, who is eighteen weeks pregnant, so we all agreed to do our own thing for dinner and meet up sometime tomorrow.

Dax and I took advantage of the buffet—and the one perk to cruising? The food. Oh my stars. So much food. And so much variety. Despite my rather lavish upbringing, we never cruised. My mom hates being on the water, so that was that.

I've heard they even have room service. So maybe that will be my vacation—reading in my room, stowed away eating food that's brought to me. Alone.

Sounds kind of nice.

Now if only we could get to said room. I wanted to go right after we ate, but Dax insisted on coming up on the deck to watch the boat pull away. I poke him. "Did you hear me?"

He moves his sunglasses down his nose, peeking out the top. Something about his eyes is shifty, but he recovers before I have a chance to ferret out what. "The weather is gorgeous, isn't it?"

I grab his arm. "You aren't telling me something."

His jaw ticks tight.

I knew it. "Dax."

Sighing, he leans against the railing and crosses his arms. "Fine, yeah. There's something I need to tell you." He waits for a second. "To show you."

I do not like his tone. Defeated. Uncomfortable. Like he's delivering bad news. But what? "Okay."

"Come on." We walk across the lido deck and toward the elevators, weaving through people who are excited to be here. Music pumps out the speakers, and guests are already swimming, some lounging on the beach chairs beside the pool. It's full vacation mode for them.

Maybe I'll get there. But my body is suddenly aching for a nap. It's six p.m. and I'm still full from our late lunch, so maybe I'll just shower, order some room service dessert, and turn in early.

We get to the elevators and hop on. Dax is bouncing a bit and swinging his arms. Have I ever seen him like this? What in the world does he need to show me? Everything has gone fairly well so far. Our brief interaction with his potential future bosses and their wives was like a little reunion, with Janet and Cecilia in their adorable matching floral maxi dresses exclaiming over my now-blue hair, giving us all hugs, introducing us to Landon and Gloria—who is flat-out gorgeous, by the way, even with her tiny baby bump.

Dax held my hand and laughed, both of us fully engaged in the conversation.

So why is he now standing there looking like he's about to come out of his skin?

After a quick descent, the elevator dings and opens. We maneuver into the rather tight hallway. The low ceiling confirms that this vessel was made to house a bunch of people in as tiny an amount of space as possible, and the hallway lined with doors every few feet makes me feel like I'm in a spaceship headed to Titan. At least the scent of coconut verbena is pleasant, if not a bit potent.

Dax reaches into his pocket and pulls out a key card, which he uses to open a door about halfway down the ship. "Here."

I peek inside. Wow, I was totally right about space saving. Sheesh. There's the world's tiniest bathroom—just a shower, sink, and toilet, and the shower looks like it's made for dwarves—plus an open closet area with a long rack, hangers, and our suitcases, which the staff brought up already. Why they didn't put my suitcase into my room is a mystery, but one easily corrected. I don't mind wheeling it down the hall myself.

Whistling, I drop onto the bed, which thankfully is super soft. "Talk about small, eh?" It's a queen but looks a lot tinier given the tight space around it—basically enough for a side table on either side, each one with a lamp and a few dresser drawers. The far wall features half of a window, revealing the striking blue ocean below. A flat-screen television hangs from the ceiling catty-corner to the bed, and underneath sits a mini-bar with two glasses and a bottle of something. I get up, take one step, and I'm there.

"Aw, look." I pick up the card propped against the bottle and wave it at Dax, who is still half in the hallway, half in the entryway. "The Bennetts got you some champagne."

He finally comes inside, shutting the door behind him. "It's for both of us."

Sure enough, the card is addressed to Dax and Alexis. I grin at him. "Maybe I'll just sneak this off to my room when you're not looking then."

He doesn't laugh. I mean, sure, I'm not as funny as him, but where's his sense of humor?

Something is definitely wrong. I squint at where he's standing, hovering between the closet area and the bedroom. "What's going on?"

"Alexis." He sighs, rubs his forehead. "There was … I tried …" Groaning, he slumps against the wall. "When I told Tom and Fred we would come on this trip, they had me talk particulars with their office manager to get everything arranged. I told her we needed two rooms. You have to believe me."

"Okay. I believe you." Why is he—

Wait.

I set the card down. "What are you saying, Dax?"

"I'm saying that *she* said she'd take care of everything. But when we checked in, I noticed we only had one room. I tried to get them to add another, but I just found out about thirty minutes ago that they're fully booked. That's the notification I got during dinner. They were waiting to see if anyone didn't show up. Apparently everyone did."

"So we're … this is …" I move my finger around the space. "*Our* room?"

My eyes stop on the bed. Oh my stars. That's *our* bed.

And there's literally nowhere else for Dax to sleep unless I make him lie down in the closet. Even that will likely be taken up largely by our suitcases. And it would be inhumane of me.

But maybe that's what he deserves.

"Alexis." He moves toward me, touches my elbow, but I yank it away. "I'm so sorry."

"You should have told me when you first found out." Given me a chance to not get on the boat at all.

"I know. You're right. I … I can just not sleep here at night. Like, I could just wander the boat or find some lounge to nap in." His lips are twisted into a frown, his forehead all scrunched. It's obvious he didn't plan this, which at least makes me feel a little better.

Until I think about having to share that tiny bed with a man who is over six feet tall. There isn't a scenario on this planet in which no part of him will not touch some part of me.

I shiver, shake it off. Straighten. "I'm not going to make you do that. We're adults, right? A-and this is a business deal. We can be professional."

"Right." He forces a laugh. "Totally. Thank you, Alexis. I'm just … so sorry."

"It's fine." I sigh and my exhaustion catches up with me as a yawn forces its way out. "You know what? We don't have to spend all that much time in here anyway." There goes my escape plan, but surely it's possible to get "lost" and "separated" from your party on a ship of this magnitude. I'll figure it out. "If you don't mind, I think I'm going to unpack and just hit the sack. Maybe read a little."

"Sure, yeah. I'll do the same."

I narrow my eyes at him. "Maybe you should go explore the deck for a while after you unpack."

He seems to catch my drift. "Good idea." Then he turns, walks to the closet, and rolls my suitcase toward the bed. "Here."

"Thanks." I heft it up onto the mattress and start working the zipper.

Meanwhile, Dax heads into the bathroom. Our bathroom.

This is so weird.

But not as weird as the feeling of my stomach bottoming out at the sight of my suitcase contents. For a second, I think I've gotten someone else's by mistake, but no, there are the five sci-fi novels I brought with me. And a note on top, written in pink ink:

Took the liberty of getting you some new threads for vacay. Don't be afraid to step out of your comfort zone. Own it like the awesome woman you are.

Someday, you'll thank me.

XOXO,

Kay

P.S. – Laughing is good for you, so I couldn't help but pack a joke item. Just remember you love me! And that I'm pregnant and not fully responsible for my actions.

So that's what Kayla was really doing with that ruck-sack—not returning Shelby's sister-in-law's clothes, but trading out mine. I'm going to murder her.

"No, no, no." I start digging around, pulling out articles of clothing that are nothing like what I would wear. Well, not true. They are bright and colorful blouses and shorts, but where are the soft Marvel T-shirts? The underwear that is admittedly a little like granny panties but also comfy because I don't have to worry about wedgies? The one-piece bathing suit (which, fine, is slightly faded in color and saggy but otherwise perfectly respectable)?

Instead, I pull out a bright red bikini—and let me just say … the fifty-dollar price tag dangling from it is nothing but a rip-off for so little material. At least Kayla included a cover-up, but of course it's white and lacy and see-through. Not much help in the modesty department.

"She's dead. Dead!"

"What?" Dax calls from the bathroom.

"Nothing!"

I keep digging. Okay, at least Kayla left the one super nice dress I own—the bridesmaid gown I wore to Evie's wedding, which will be perfect for the formal dinner night on board. But still. Everything else, including the baggy shirt and basketball shorts I normally wear to bed, has been replaced.

Huffing out a laugh of disbelief, I fist my hand around a pile of colorful silky underwear in a boy-short style, and—what in the cosmic cube is this atrocity? I hold up some sort of black, lacy, frilly bodysuit.

I couldn't help but pack a joke item.

Oh, yeah. I don't care that she's in a "fragile state." Kayla Gregory is going down.

Like the bikini, there isn't much to this thing, but it's clearly not meant for public consumption, thanks to its see-through nature, the plunging neckline, and the—I squeak—cheek exposure in back.

"Whoa."

Whirling, I clutch the lingerie to my chest.

Dax is standing behind me, staring at Kayla's "gift," his mouth flopping open. "Um."

"It's …" My heartbeat is going haywire and I shove the lingerie behind me, back into the depths of the suitcase. "Not what it looks like."

"What it looks like is you brought sexy lingerie on our trip."

I cringe. "Okay, so it is what it looks like, technically. But it was my friend. She's a dating coach and can't help but try to pair people up." What? Why did I say that? Kayla didn't mean for me to *actually* make use of this thing. It's a joke. But how to convince Dax of that?

"Oh, yeah?" Dax is over the awkwardness of the moment already, folding his arms over his chest, leaning against the wall, smirking. "Why would she try to pair us up? She doesn't even know me."

"She thinks I think …" Nope, not going there. Dax doesn't need any more inflation to his ego. "Can we just get back to unpacking please?"

"Go right ahead." He peeks over my shoulder. "I'm curious to see what other gems *your friend* packed." He emphasizes "your friend" like he doesn't believe it really was my friend.

"*I* didn't pack this!"

"It's okay to admit you're attracted to me, Alexis." He's laughing now. Then he steps forward, lowers his mouth to my ear. "But we're just pretending, remember?" There's maybe a real question there, in his tease, but just like the thought of what he's not saying, I push him away. My hands stay on his chest, fingers flexing, just a second longer than necessary. *Why does he have to be so darn attractive?*

"Of course I remember," I manage, dropping my hands. "Now go finish unpacking and explore the ship so I can sleep. I don't want to be in your presence any longer than I have to be."

"Aye, aye, Captain." He salutes and starts whistling as he disappears around the corner and gets to work on his suitcase zipper.

My insides quivering, I sink onto the bed and eye my clothing. This is a disaster. I can't wear this stuff. But what other choice do I have? Tomorrow we're at sea all day, and it's not like I'm going to spend my precious money on new clothing in St. Thomas or Barbados.

I'm just going to have to suck it up and own these clothing choices Kayla made for me (well, clearly not ALL of them). But as soon as I have access to my phone again, you'd better believe she's getting a severe tongue lashing.

Dax is humming *Here Comes the Sun* and the scrape of hangers against metal fills the air. While he's distracted, I find what I think is supposed to be my sleepwear—a silky black pajama set with tiny shorts and a tank top that's a bit low for my liking—and my toiletries bag and head to the bathroom. While I shower, I try to avoid thinking about this predicament I'm in. Try to hold onto my anger at Dax for not telling me about the one-room situation. Try to remember why I'm here.

My job. The house. Kennedy.

I let the warm water wash away the negativity of the day and by the time I'm done, I'm looking forward to snuggling up in bed—by myself—and reading until I fall asleep.

But even after the lights are out and my body sinks into the mattress and I read for two hours, sleep doesn't come. My eyes are finally starting to close when the door to our cabin opens, shuts. It must be Dax. I pretend to be asleep, but there's definitely no sleeping now that I know he's headed in this direction.

There's a bit of a reprieve while he goes into the bathroom. I hear the water thump on and there's a good fifteen minutes I just lie there, staring at the ceiling, wondering how I landed myself here—about to share a bed with a man. Not that I'm worried anything will happen, but sleeping in the same room is an intimate thing.

A vulnerable thing.

And I don't want to be vulnerable with Dax. All the revelations I had with my friends the other day? Nope. I'm not ready for them after all. It's one thing to trust friends who have proven their loyalty time and again. It's another to possibly trust another guy with my heart.

Especially one who might be leaving, if we play our parts well.

Why is my mind even bending in that direction? I. Do. Not. Like. This. Man. Not even as a person. Not even as a friend. Definitely not as more than that.

The shower turns off and I can hear Dax shuffling around in the bathroom. My blood is whooshing in my ears as I turn onto my side, away from the middle of the bed, close my eyes, and pray for sleep to find me. I keep the curtains open so the moonlight can filter in, can remind me that I am still the same Alexis—that this is still the same sky as always.

Nothing has changed.

I smell him before I feel the dip of the mattress. The hints of cinnamon are there, but overpowered by a spicy citrus and bergamot aroma that turns my stomach with the way my toes curl in response. Darn him and his amazing body wash.

"Alexis?" he whispers. "Are you awake?"

Determined not to answer, I grip the comforter at my chest. He sighs and the mattress moves with him as he lies down beside me. Immediately, I am warmer. I hate that. I don't want his warmth. I can warm myself.

We stay like that for a while, both of us awake, not sleeping, but eventually his breathing becomes even, steady. It's a full ten minutes before I get the courage to move, to peek at him.

Holy stars.

He's asleep all right, but the comforter is only half covering his body. His very naked body, at least from the waist up. Why didn't he wear a shirt? Is he trying to give me a heart attack? To prove something? To taunt me?

I've never seen Dax with his shirt off, and it feels wrong to ogle him in his sleep, but it's like when you go into an art museum and see something truly magnificent—you just have to study the masterpiece.

Every ridge, every swoop of skin, every muscle sculpted even when relaxed. The light dusting of dark hair skates across his pectorals, down the center of his chest, leading all the way through his pack of abs down to the band of his shorts—and it is happy indeed.

Okay, I'm officially a creeper and now it's too hot in here to sleep. I duck out from beneath the comforter and head to the bathroom, where I sit on the toilet, bow my head into my hands, and stifle a scream.

I cannot with these … feelings.

I've been around hot guys before. So what is it about Dax Nyhart that has my blood boiling—in both good and bad ways? Suddenly, disappearing tomorrow, hiding out, sounds like the perfect way to get back my equilibrium.

One day at a time. That's the only way I'll survive this torture.

nine

THIS IS UNREAL.

I lay my head back, the sun warm on my face, my body stretched out on a deck chair. A book sits open across my lap, and I keep nodding off after getting only about four hours of sleep.

But if I want to sleep, I can sleep. It's a Monday afternoon and I'm not working. Instead, I'm sitting by a pool that seems from my vantage point to meet the ocean at the edge of the cruise ship. Alone but not (given all the other cruise ship guests here), I'm not at the main pool —there are five—but the one at the back of the ship, so I can see where we've been instead of where we're going. And I'm okay with that. Okay with sitting here, smelling the sea air. Hearing the call of gulls over the Carly Rae Jepsen song playing on the ship's speakers.

Not working.

It's glorious, really.

And the best part? My emotions are fully in check. I

haven't even seen Dax this morning. After my fitful night, I woke up to a stateroom empty of all but a breakfast tray on the mini-bar and a note from Dax saying he went to the gym and would see me later. Putting my plan into action, I downed the eggs, bacon, and fruit and tossed on (not without a grimace) the bikini and coverup Kayla packed me. Then I stuffed my sunglasses, some sunscreen, my room card, and my book into a beach bag and made my way up to the chair I've been occupying for several hours, only getting up once to use the restroom and snag a slice of pizza for lunch.

I'm not so naive that I think I can get away with this the entire trip, but it's nice to lose myself in someone's story other than my own. I take a sip of my strawberry daiquiri and crack open the book again, settle into the story which—much to Evie's chagrin—is anything but a romance.

"Yoohoo! Alexis!"

I flinch at the sound of Janet's voice and turn to the entire horde of Bennett Toys employees, spouses, and potential future employees traipsing up the steps toward me—including Dax. Janet and Cecilia wave, the brims of their ginormous beach hats blowing in the slight breeze. Everyone is dressed in pool gear, from Gloria's tankini to Janet and Cecilia's red coverups to Tom and Fred's extremely hairy chests that look like wooly shirts. Dax is casual in his swim trunks, his sunglasses hooked onto the front of his white T-shirt.

"There you are, darling!" Cecilia sets her beach bag down beside my chair and the whole group crowds around me.

"Hey, guys." I flash an apologetic look at the family with two kids to my left.

The mom catches my eye and smiles as she reaches for a bottle of sunscreen on the deck. "Excuse me," she says, and our group turns. "We're just about to leave if y'all want these seats."

Great. I'd hoped we'd chat for a few minutes and they'd go on to do their thing, but given their squeals of thanks and delight, it looks like I'm about to get new neighbors.

Dax drops onto the bottom half of my chair facing me and places his hand on my ankle.

My eyes shoot to his at the contact and I'm about to rip him a new one for his inappropriate touching, but he side-eyes Landon and Gloria, who are both staring adoringly at her belly, stroking it as they talk with Tom and Fred about the elation over their impending arrival.

Okay, I get it. Dax needs his wingman. Wingwoman. Whatever.

I place my book in my bag and lean forward, my voice low. "Hard to compete with a baby."

"Guess we've got our work cut out for us, huh?" He's staring at my ankle now, and his thumb flits over the bone in a smooth circle that leaves me a bit breathless.

"Guess so." I'm proud of myself for managing that much.

While our group waits for the other chairs to clear, Dax and I stand and walk hand in hand toward Landon and Gloria. From our limited interaction, I've learned that the parents of three are Los Angeles natives and have a 2-, 5-, and 7-year-old. They're probably a bit older than Dax and me—I'd say late thirties instead of early—and Gloria's lithe body, lightly tanned skin, dark brown eyes, and dark hair that's straight and long make her look like a flipping goddess and the direct opposite of Landon, a redhead who's on the shorter side (though not shorter than Gloria) and a bit paunchy, with glasses and skin that's paler than Shelby's. He looks like he'd turn from man to lobster in no time flat if he stayed out here very long.

"Have you had a nice morning?" Gloria asks in her lilting accent splashed with hints of her Mexican-American heritage.

"Yep, just taking advantage of the time to read." I learned yesterday that Fred and Tom have some excursions planned this week, so I'm going to enjoy the relaxation while I can.

"I'm surprised to find you alone." She eyes my now-empty chair. "Landon and I plan to spend every minute together we possibly can, right, sweetie?"

He startles and looks away from Tom, Fred, and their wives, who are busy settling into their seats. "What?" He nods. "Oh, yes. Of course."

Gloria frowns for a split second, then flashes her pearly whites and places her hand—once again—on her baby bump. I mean, Evie and Kayla do touch their stomachs a lot, but I get the sense that's in a loving way.

This placement feels like a trump card.

"Maybe when *you* are parents, you'll understand how important it is to spend as much time together as possible," she coos.

Yeah. Definitely don't like her tone *or* what she's implying. I open my mouth for a retort, but before I can make it, Dax slides his arm around my waist and tugs me to him.

I freeze and, stars, he smells good. Sunscreen mixed with cinnamon—it's now a thing and I will forever love it. I can't help but melt into him a little bit.

He chuckles at my reaction and my cheeks warm. "My little JuJuBee here just values her independence. It's something I love about her."

I feel the rumble of his chest as he speaks, and I wonder if there's any truth in his statement. A man who would actually like independence in a woman? No, that can't be real. My mom depended on my dad for everything and he loved it, soaked up her company when he was home. He just didn't like it when she would beg to accompany him on his work trips, would always say they couldn't pull me out of school, et cetera et cetera, and that he believed she could hold down the fort while he was away.

I mean, now I know why he really couldn't let her come with him. He was visiting his other family.

But at the time, I thought it adorable how much he wished she could come. How he promised to make the trip quick so they could be together again.

It's disgusting when you think about it, stringing two women along like that.

The thought sours my tastebuds and I force myself to laugh along with everyone else. When Janet, Cecilia, and company join the circle, they tell us they're buying drinks for all—though virgin for Gloria, of course!—and we place our orders before sitting. Then Landon and Gloria share the chair beside mine and Dax's seat (there weren't quite enough for us all to have our own), and everyone starts peeling off their coverups and shirts.

Including Dax.

We're sitting side by side, and I try to avert my eyes but can't help the magnetism of his body in full light—plus I can play it off as admiring him for the sake of our little fake engagement charade. Of course, that doesn't stop my cheeks from igniting again when he catches me staring.

"Like what you see, RB?" His husky voice bridges the space between us and his eyebrows spike upward in teasing. He's as smug as he is sexy with his non-gelled hair sticking up a bit behind his ear and his tan skin, and I want to do something to knock him down a peg, make sure he doesn't have the upper hand.

So it's my turn to peel off my coverup. "Do you?"

By the looks of him—eyes suddenly wide, pupils dilated, tongue running along his top teeth underneath his lip—I'd say he does.

There's a weird flicker of satisfied power that comes with the knowledge that I affect him. And I'm not quite sure what to do with that.

Gloria's giggle from the next chair over snaps us both out of our staring competition. "Dax, you're looking at her like you've never seen her in a bathing suit before. Don't you guys live together?"

Oh, the implications of *that* statement. Dax blinks a few times in rapid succession, then his shoulders relax as he's back to putting on an act.

"But we're just pretending, remember?" His words from last night float back to me.

We might be pretending, but he can't deny what I just saw in his eyes. Flagrant interest. Appreciation at the very least.

Not that I would ask him, because then he might pester me about seeing the same thing in my gaze.

But this is not the time to think about that (that time is NEVER) because Gloria's question requires a response. "We don't live together, actually. And he's staring because this is a new bathing suit."

"Ah." She smiles, then nudges Landon to turn around, put his back to her. "Babe, hand me the sunscreen. You're going to burn to a crisp." Then she nods at me, her eyes twinkling. "You'd better let Dax get your back, Alexis. You're looking quite pink already."

My eyes snap to Dax's and he shrugs. I swivel and swing my leg over the side so now I'm facing the pool, sitting in front of him.

"Scoot back a little farther," he says, his voice a bit hoarse.

I peek over my shoulder at him and he's frowning as he stares at my braid, which is clearly in the way. Lifting it, I pull it to the front of my body, clearing a path for the sunscreen.

For his hands.

Don't think about it, don't think about it, don't think—

My breath hitches as the cool sunscreen hits my hot skin. At his fingers as they lightly skim the cream across the top of my shoulders, down my back. His fingers' brush leaves a fiery trail of detonating nerves and I realize with a start that no one has touched me like this in years. Not since Corbin.

And it's like awareness is coming back to life with every stroke, every caress, every kiss of his skin against mine. When his fingers shift one strap of my bathing suit a fraction of an inch to the left, I grip the edge of the chair under my legs and nearly come out of my seat. But then he rubs sunscreen in the spot and moves the strap back where it belongs.

Still, I can't suppress a shiver.

Dax leans forward and his chest presses lightly against my back. "Cold, RB?"

Quite hot actually. I hop up. "You wish." Then I race to the pool and cannonball in, grateful when the cold water douses my skin.

But it's going to take more than that to cool the racing heat inside of me.

Because I cannot deny the attraction any longer. It's there. I'm only human, after all. What woman wouldn't be attracted to him, especially if she had to lie in bed next to him all night?

But you know what? That's part of life. As long as it doesn't go farther than appreciating the pure manliness of Dax Nyhart, it's not a problem. As long as the heat doesn't burn away the lock that's on my heart, we're golden.

"Is the water cold, dear?" Cecilia calls.

"No." I flash a thumbs-up to them all. "It's perfect."

Just perfect.

I haven't been clubbing since—yeah, never.

And I find it quite hilarious that my first time is with four fifty-somethings, two strangers I met just yesterday, and my mortal enemy-slash-fake fiancé.

Also hilarious is the fact that a cruise ship has such a wide variety of entertainment. It's only nine p.m. and we've already eaten dinner (at the crazy early hour of five, because of said fifty-somethings), played a few slots in the on-ship casino, and listened to the end of a comedian's bit.

Now I'm sitting with Dax, Landon, and Gloria at a table on the edge of the nightclub watching Janet and Cecilia having a ball dancing with their husbands under the glass roof that's been retracted. Long sheer white draperies cover the windows that flank the dance floor, blowing in the breeze drifting in from above. A DJ spins in the corner, his current pick a number I don't recognize. The dance floor is crowded but not overly full. Outside, the stars have joined the moon, and it's the perfect night to relax.

And maybe I would if Dax wasn't so nearby, looking so handsome in a blazer, jeans, and a collared shirt with the top button undone and a tiny triangle of tan skin peeking out the top. The whole thing is a tease and I do not like my body's reaction to it. It inspires … thoughts.

So I sit here, legs crossed, biting into my straw as I

down some fruity blue beverage Gloria brought me, saying I had to drink it for her because she can't.

"Aren't you guys going to dance?" Gloria points between Dax and me, eyebrow raised.

"Oh, um." I glance up, take another desperate sip of my drink, which unfortunately answers with an almost empty slurp. "Well, what about you?"

"It's too crowded out there." Landon puts his arm around his wife and squeezes her shoulders. "Don't want the baby to get jostled."

Gloria smiles, but there's something strained in it. "Yeah, but don't let us stop you guys from going out there. Getting your groove thing on." She groans. "Listen to me. I'm a decrepit old mom now. So not hip."

"If it helps, I'm not hip either," I say. "And I don't mind sitting out."

Dax has been a bit on the quiet side all evening—and maybe it's because when we got back to our room after the pool, I snapped at him for leaving the toilet seat up and the disastrous state of the bathroom. And yes, I realize I may be slightly anal about things because I haven't had to share a bathroom with anyone for a very long time (my roommates share the hallway one, while I have the master), but I think I also was trying to not think about the fact he would be showering minutes after I was.

Picking a fight felt normal, restored our dynamic a bit.

But he didn't seem to enjoy it as much as I did. Just got quiet, apologized, and cleaned up the bathroom.

Now, he's sitting here, leaning forward in his seat,

feet planted shoulder width apart as he finishes off his Jack and Coke. Before I can say anything else, he stands and sets the empty glass on the table. Holds out his hand to me. "Come on. Let's show everyone what we're made of."

His gaze holds mine steady, and there's a challenge in it. I can't read him, but it's not like the mask he always wears at work. It's different. More nuanced.

And tonight, after fighting my attraction for him all day, I can't handle figuring it out. "Sorry, I need to use the restroom." Then I scoot out of the booth and practically run in these stupid heels Kayla packed for me into the bathroom on the other side of the club.

The pulse of the music shakes the stall doors ever so slightly. I grab one and dash inside the stall, shutting myself away and inhaling deep breaths—which I come to regret because, you know, it's a bathroom. After using the restroom (might as well while I'm here), I exit the stall to find Gloria sitting on the loveseat by the door.

Well, that's not creepy at all.

"Hey," she says in this soothing voice that sounds sticky-sweet. I'm not sure if it's sincere.

"Hi." My greeting is short and clipped as I wash my hands. "You okay?"

"Just checking on you." She pats the cushioned seat next to her. "You ran out of there pretty quickly."

"Just really needed to go." I click my back teeth together. There's nothing for it but to take the spot she's offering me. I guess this is still a form of hiding out, albeit with company, but I'll take it. "I'm fine if you want to rejoin your husband. I know you're cherishing every moment." I try desperately to sound perky, totally fine, and not sarcastic at all.

But Gloria studies me so intently that I'm pretty sure I've failed. She starts to open her mouth to speak, but a few drunk twenty-somethings stumble in, continuing their dance moves and giggling all the way to their stalls. Their laughter reminds me of my friends and I can't help but smile.

"There it is."

"What?"

"A smile. I've been waiting all day to see one."

Why has she been watching me so closely? We aren't even friends. Technically, we're kind of rivals for the same jobs—well, our men are. Not that Dax is my man, but everyone thinks he is. (Just stating how it would appear from Gloria's point of view, okay? Oy, this is more exhausting than I thought it would be.)

"I'm just tired from all the travel the last few days."

"Are you sure that's it?" She bites her lip, hesitates, then takes my hand. Hers is smooth and cool and tiny in mine. What's happening here? Is she momming me?

"Um, yes?"

"Because I can't help but notice that you seem the tensest when Dax is around. I never see you initiate contact with him, and I know when Landon and I were engaged, we couldn't keep our hands off of each other."

Well, that's not good. "Oh, I'm just not that affectionate of a person." I pause, shift in my seat. "And we had a fight earlier over something stupid. You know." Shrugging, I roll my eyes. "Couples stuff."

"I just wanted to …" She inhales, holds the bridge of

her nose. "Wanted to be sure he was good to you. You deserve someone who sees the beauty of your soul, Alexis."

Whaaaaaat? Okay, lady. "You don't even know me." I pull my hand away, not bothering to make it gentle but a straight-up tug. "And Dax is good to me. Great, in fact. He's … he's wonderful." Okay, it's maybe stretching the truth a bit for the guy who irritates me to no end.

Although … is it? For all his obnoxious behavior, have I ever seen him degrade someone else? Truly? Or do I just have such a strong aversion to men in general that I've made his flaws bigger in my mind than they really are?

Regardless of what is reality, I've got to prove to Gloria that I'm in love with Dax, because right now, she's clearly not convinced. And if she's not convinced, it's possible that the Bennetts aren't either. They won't hire Dax if they don't believe he's a solid family man—and I've got to leave them with no doubts.

"Thanks for your concern, but I think I'll go dance with my fiancé now." I dart out of my seat and don't wait for her to catch up with me as I make it to the edge of dance floor, swooping my gaze across it before it lands on Dax dancing sweetly with Cecilia.

My heart is hammering in my ears. I know what I have to do.

"Here, love." Like a spirit, Janet appears beside me in her flowing white sundress. She shoves some sort of green martini into my hand. "You look like you could use this."

"Bless you." I take the drink and down the whole thing, barely tasting the alcohol and fruit mixture before giving her back the empty glass.

"Now go make up with your man." Janet winks.

Ugh, I was right. Even she thinks something is wrong between us. My stomach twists and I nod, then force myself across the dance floor as "Hideaway" plays. The bass pounds under my feet, in time to my heart. Dax is patting Cecilia on the back, leading her off the dance floor when she says something to him and they both look at me.

But I only see him.

"You can do this, you can do this," I whisper to myself.

Then I walk right up to Dax Nyhart and kiss him hard on the mouth.

He's stiff for a second or two before his hands fall to my waist. Mine are glued to his cheeks as our lips move together, and oh my stars, they are warm and soft and taste like the fizz of Coca-Cola, the bite of Jack Daniels—the sweetness of Dax.

One of his hands moves into my hair before his groan brings me swiftly back to reality and I pull away. For what feels like a full minute, we stand there, blinking at each other. As the music swirls around us, he runs his hand through his hair. "Wow, um." Cough. "What was that for?"

I peek out of the corner of my eye and see our group all watching us. Janet and Cecilia are clapping, Tom and Fred laugh, Landon looks bored, and Gloria stands there tightlipped. "For our audience."

"Ah." His eyes fill with understanding. "Our cover was in trouble, then?"

"Why else would I have kissed you?" *Why else indeed?*

"Dance with her!" Janet shouts from across the room. She shakes her voluptuous hips and her breasts threaten to jiggle right out the top of her low-cut dress.

Dax chuckles, then tilts his ear toward the DJ's booth. "This song sounds about right, you know."

I start to listen—actually listen—and recognize the song. "'Shut Up and Dance'?"

"Yep." He starts to bounce to the rhythm. "It's perfect for you."

"I don't dance."

"Yeah, but you do like to boss me around." His shoulders roll from one side to the other like he's doing the snake.

"That doesn't mean I dance." But I can't help the inch of a smile at the corner of my mouth because Dax is starting to look ridiculous as he croons about this woman being his destiny. Then he holds his hand out to me like he's gripping an invisible mic. I push it away.

He places his hands on my hips and starts to sway me back and forth.

I let my arms droop pathetically at my sides, but he doesn't relent, just swings me a bit harder and my hands are flying, swinging like I'm a life-size rag doll. The way his eyes are lit up, all playful and adorable, makes me want to give in and dance with the guy.

I can let go for one dance, can't I? I've been so wound up tight for years. One dance. It won't kill me.

The chorus of the song comes on and suddenly I jerk to life, grabbing his hand and singing into it that he'd better shut up and dance with me.

And then he does. We do. We're ridiculous with our moves—because honestly, I *can't* dance—but it doesn't matter how silly we are. He spins me in and out, our fingers connecting and releasing. My arms curl above my head like I'm reaching for the stars looking down on us, and my hips move to the beat, my braid whipping against my lower back until Dax slides his hand around me again.

This feels … I don't even know.

Like freedom. A taste of it, anyway. And when the Bennetts join us, we're a raucous crew shouting lyrics at each other as one song fades into the next.

I almost don't notice Dax tugging at the collar of his shirt. Looking a bit paler. Clutching his stomach. Stopping.

But when I do, I pull him to the side. "You okay?"

"My throat is tingly. My stomach … it doesn't feel right. I don't understand. I've only ever felt this way when …" Then he glances up at me, a sharp look in his eye. "Alexis, did you have anything with kiwis in it?"

Kiwis? "No." Wait. "Maybe? Janet gave me a green drink just before …"

"Before we kissed."

I nod.

His eyes widen and he pats his pockets frantically. "I'm allergic." A curse. "And apparently I've forgotten my epi-pen back in the room. I never do that."

"Dax!"

"I know!"

"Ugh. You're the worst!" Then I grab his hand and we take off running to find the medical bay before the man I'm discovering maybe isn't so bad keels over and dies.

ten

. . .

OKAY, turns out not everyone with a food allergy becomes deathly ill when they ingest said food. Some just get hives and puke their guts out.

Ask me how I know this.

After the physician on staff gave Dax a dose of epinephrine and observed him for a while, we returned to our room. Now I'm lying on our bed feeling like the worst sort of person. I did this to Dax. Because I gave him the Kiwi Kiss of Death without warning. A few minutes ago, he started to assure me that it's not a big deal—but then rushed off to the bathroom to hurl. Again.

I click on the television and mindlessly watch the cruise network's channel as I wait for him to emerge. There are visions of laughing people kicking up sand as they run hand in hand across the perfect white beach. Floating on huge tubes down rivers. Sunbathing under a cabana on canary-yellow towels.

Even though we will likely be doing some of that tomorrow on St. Thomas—so long as Dax is feeling better—none of it feels real. It's an illusion, cast out there into the universe, reeling people in with its bright and sunny pictures of a life that isn't authentic. Those are just actors, and when the shoot was over, they went back to their lives, probably in a beat-up apartment where they live with five other people in a room no bigger than a closet.

Is there anything really that good, that pure, that happy in the world?

I know it seems like my friends have found it. They really do seem at peace, in love. But will it last? I pray for their sakes that it will. Maybe they simply have more capacity to love than I do. Maybe it's not men who are the problem.

Maybe it's me.

The sliver of truth—the question in it—needles through the bricks in my fortress, poking and prodding where I do not want it.

And all because of some lies the TV told me.

I huff and start to turn it off, but am startled by the opening of the bathroom door. Poor Dax. He looks miserable. His lips are still puffy, although definitely better than they were when they started to swell. The doctor said the symptoms should resolve soon but that I should observe him off and on through the night if we're worried.

"Hey." I scooch closer to the edge of the bed, allowing him more room than normal. "How are you feeling?"

"Like death." He tries to chuckle but it comes out as a coughing bark. Then he plops onto the bed and stretches out. His leg hits mine and he winces. "Sorry."

"Don't worry about it." I reach over and get a water bottle off my side table. "Here. You should drink this."

"Not sure I can manage it."

"You've got to try. I won't have you getting dehydrated on my watch."

"Yes, ma'am," Dax croaks. He tries to sit up and open the lid, but just kind of wriggles and then lets his hand drop, the bottle with it.

I snag it and twist the top open, holding it to his lips. "Drink."

His eyes pop up to mine and he does what I demand, his gaze never leaving me. When he's done, he lays his head back against the pillows. "Did I just drink poisoned water?"

"What?" Why in the world is he asking that? I set the water bottle on the table again and half-lay-half-sit back against my pillow. "No."

"Good." He closes his eyes, putting his arm across them. "You've just never been this nice to me before. I should try almost dying more often."

"You'd better not." Laughing, I kick at his bare foot. At the contact, his responds, moving back to mine, resting against it. We don't move again, just let our feet lay there together, the only part of us touching.

So basically, my foot is on fire. Yep.

I cough. "Want to watch something?"

"Sure, until I have to get up and barf again."

"Sexy."

"That's me. Sexiest man alive."

Rolling my eyes, I turn up the TV volume and start to flip through the options available. "Just say when." The channels roll over from one action movie to another, a few that look interesting enough I would have stopped, but this is Dax's rodeo.

Still, at his "When" on *10 Things I Hate About You*, I do a double take. "I'm sorry?"

"When." He finally uncovers his eyes and looks at the TV. "I love this movie."

"It's a rom-com."

"Yeah, so?"

"A *chick* flick."

"That's so sexist, Alexis." His foot nudges mine again. "Guys can like rom-coms."

"I guess." I set the remote on the bed between us, allowing myself to sink into the mattress. "Just don't watch this on my account."

"Not a romance fan?" Grabbing one of the pillows from under his head, he turns on his side and hugs it to his chest. Looks at me.

I grab my braid. Fidget. "Not particularly."

There's silence for a bit while we watch a drunk, concussed Julia Stiles and Heath Ledger on some swings. But Dax picks up the remote and mutes it before we get too far. "Why not?"

"Huh?"

"Why aren't you a romance fan?"

"I prefer things with more action. Blood. Battles." I unmute the TV and it roars to life again.

"Makes sense. You do like to fight."

"Ha ha, so funny." I pause. "The question is why are *you* a romance fan?"

But he answers my question by muting the screen yet again. I'm surprised the neighbors don't pound on the wall in annoyance, but maybe the walls are actually thicker than they appear from the hallway.

Then he waits.

I don't owe him anything, really. Except. Ugh. I guess I do, given I'm the reason he's crumpled into the fetal position. "I don't like to watch rom-coms because they perpetuate the lie about love."

"And what lie is that?"

"That it lasts. That there is someone out there for everyone. That there are soulmates." I believed my parents were meant to be, that Corbin and I were—but apparently both my dad and my ex had more than one soulmate. "I'd think you would understand better than anyone after what happened with Lilith."

"Alexis, you don't know what happened with Lilith." He readjusts so he can look up at me, but he's clearly craning his neck too far.

So he can see me better—and more comfortably—I slide down so we are lying on our sides facing each other. "I guess you're right."

"Ladies and gentlemen, you heard it here first. Alexis Matkin thinks I'm right."

I tuck the pillow under my chin, roll my eyes at his dramatics. "I'm only saying that because you're sick. Tomorrow I go back to being right."

"I'm going to make tonight stretch on, then." He's

quiet for a bit as his green eyes study mine. "Lilith and I
…"

"You don't have to tell me." Part of me prays he
flicks the show back on. Because honestly, where can all
of this lead? Neither of us want a relationship. I don't
trust him. So what's the point in getting to know him?

And yet.

"It's okay," he says. "I … want to."

"Okay."

A noisy someone walks down our hallway, where a
light shines just under the doorway, but they pass soon
enough. Then it's just me and him and the air
between us.

"When we first got together, I thought I'd won the
lottery, you know? She's that kind of girl. Smart, beautiful. Ambitious. Larger than life in a lot of ways, some of
which could be cruel and cutting. Things I didn't see
until it was too late."

"Like what?"

Dax studies me for a few long seconds before answering. "She said mean things about other people. And me.
Backhanded compliments, you know? Oh, and she'd be
upset for no reason." His chuckle is dry and strained. "I
spent so much time trying to make things up to her, even
though I didn't know what things I'd done wrong."

"Sounds manipulative."

He sighs. "Yeah, I guess so. She just played a lot of
mind games, you know?" The air crackles and bends as
he shifts a bit, settles in some more. "The next woman I
date …"

I bite the inside of my lower lip. Wait for him to continue.

"I want someone who tells me what she's thinking, who doesn't pretend to be upset if she isn't, who I can read. Someone who is honest almost to a fault."

"That's something I admire about you, Alexis. You always tell it like it is. Even when people don't want to hear it." His words outside the pizza restaurant just before our fake date drift back to me.

My thighs clench. Is he saying …?

But what I'm realizing in this moment is he's wrong about me. I'm willing to bet he has no idea what's going through my mind right now. There are so many things I haven't told him—like how I can't stop thinking about our kiss earlier tonight. How I wished we hadn't been in public, could have explored more of this growing attraction between us.

I've silently accused Dax of wearing a mask, of always being happy in public, and yet I've been the opposite, cursing his name and being belligerent and sarcastic while hiding this brimming *something* under the surface. And maybe that makes me just as bad as Dax. Maybe withholding the truth is nearly as damaging as lying.

Oh my gosh. I'm *such* a hypocrite.

And yet, I don't know what to do with these feelings he's starting to raise in me. This can't go anywhere. I can't trust it to. And I know that.

But still. I can't deny that, in this moment, in the dimness of the room, beneath my chest there pulses a heart that's trying to break free again. Trying to find a piece of myself that I lost so many years ago.

And I'm terrified of both finding it and declaring it lost forever.

I realize Dax is staring at me—or more accurately, at my lip, which I am gnawing so hard I'm surprised it's not bleeding. Clearing my throat, I blink. "So, what happened? With Lilith, I mean?"

"Oh." He blinks too, and I sense that his mind might have gone astray as well. Is *he* thinking about our kiss? "We'd been growing apart for a while. Had been engaged for two years, but the whole time, she couldn't decide on anything related to the wedding. Except she really wanted a big flashy honeymoon in Fiji."

"Hmm. Fiji is beautiful." I desperately need to get our equilibrium back here, so I try for a tease. "Can't blame a girl."

He chuckles. "I didn't. But the fact I could never pin her down on a wedding date, flowers, even wedding attendants, was concerning. Finally, I confronted her about it. It was right after you met her, actually."

"That was a treat." I'd run into her at the snack stand during Shelby's musical, where she'd proceeded to tell me I shouldn't order an oatmeal pie because of the high calorie count. So of course, that's exactly what I bought —and then accidentally ran into Dax's chest with it.

"You ruined that shirt, by the way. It was never the same after the creaming."

I laugh. "Yeah, well, you ruined my pie."

The warmth of his foot finds mine again, and this time his toes flex against my skin, effectively stroking my instep. Ack. I swear I am *not* a foot person, so why is this tiny contact making my nerves short circuit?

The funny thing? His face doesn't betray a thing, and I try to keep mine stoic as well. We are like boiling pots of water with the lids on. Lots of steam fogging up the top, an explosion waiting to happen. But not yet.

I clear my throat. "So, you confronted her." Yes, good. Get the convo back on track.

You could just roll over and go to sleep, Alexis. You don't have to get to know him better. That will only lead to a place you aren't willing to go.

My subconscious is right. And yet there's something sitting on a corner of the fortress around my heart, and it's a heavy something, so heavy it's making one of the bricks crumble. And all I can do is watch on in equal parts horror and fascination.

And maybe, a tiny bit of hope.

"After I confronted her, she said she didn't want to set a date until we'd finalized what we were doing after the wedding. She wanted to move to New York City, found the San Diego scene boring. Found our life boring, I guess." He reaches up, scratches behind his ear.

"Why didn't you want to go to New York?"

"First of all, my mom is here. Moving to Los Angeles would be one thing, but she … well, anyway, I didn't want to leave her."

Now that he mentions his mother, I remember her calling when he drove us to the airport. I didn't hear her side of the conversation, but I do remember him detailing when he'd be home, when he'd be out of service, and reminding her that Nate was available if she needed someone. He white-knuckled the steering wheel with one hand and I slipped my AirPods in and listened to a murder mystery podcast the rest of the drive.

Maybe she's super controlling, just like Lilith was. Not sure if that's better or worse than mine, who didn't seem to mind when I moved all the way across the country.

"Ah, so you're a mama's boy, then?" I tease. His jaw flinches and I can see I've touched a nerve. "I'm just kidding," I say softly.

"It's okay." He shakes his head. "She's struggled with a pain pill addiction for years after a work injury that put her on disability when I was a teen."

"Oh my goodness. I'm such a jerk."

That puts a smile—albeit a small one—on his face. "You're not so bad." Then after a deep exhale, "Over the years, she's had some relapses, went to rehab a few times. Now she's working her program, so she's okay, but she's kind of in a delicate state. Nate helps out, but he's got his own career, his own family to worry about. I don't want to be far if I can help it. Lilith didn't seem to understand that, so I let her go."

Wow. That's a lot to unpack. "I'm sorry." And I am.

"It all worked out in the end. Honestly, it was awful for the first few weeks, but I quickly realized I wasn't actually in love with her anymore, if I ever was. I may have thought I'd won the jackpot, but I was playing the wrong game."

Oddly, this makes so much sense to me. "So after

that experience, what is it that makes you still believe in love? So much that you not only tolerate watching rom-coms, but actually enjoy them?"

He must catch the tease in my tone because Dax laughs.

But I'm actually kind of serious. "Your parents must have a great love story, right?"

"Actually, my dad walked out when I was ten. Just out of the blue left a note saying he had to go."

"Ugh, that stinks." It's such an inadequate word for the situation, but I don't know what else to say.

He fingers the edge of the pillowcase. "You know what he said in his note? That now it was my turn to be the man of the house since he couldn't be. So that's what I did. Worked any job I could—babysitting, paper route, then the bigger leagues like McDonald's and Office Depot—just to pay the rent. We had food stamps, but the rest of Mom's disability checks didn't really cover much beyond some medical bills and a junky old car."

"Dax. That's amazing." I seriously don't know what to say. There is so much more depth to him than I let myself see.

And frankly? It scares me.

Because I can't help but feel like a man who supports his mom like Dax does would make an incredible boyfriend. Fiancé. Husband.

For someone else, obviously. But still.

"It's not amazing. Isn't it just normal?"

"You'd be surprised," I murmur.

His forehead creases slightly, a line right between his two brows. "I just take care of my people, Alexis. When

I can, anyway. Back then, work and school and helping Mom with her meds—it was too much, I guess, because I was driving home at midnight one night after a shift and fell asleep at the wheel. When Uncle Nate finally saw what was going on, he stepped up and helped us out financially. Put me through college, found me an awesome internship, eventually a job at his company when he had the bandwidth to take on another employee."

"You're lucky to have an uncle who cares about you so much."

"I know. But it's not his responsibility, you know? It's mine. I'm the one who should be the man of the house that my father couldn't be. My mom, she's all alone, and I need to buy the house she's in. The landlord told her several months ago that he needs to sell it, and there's no way I can afford it without a drastic raise. It's where I grew up, where she's most comfortable."

"What about Nate? Wouldn't he help out?"

"He doesn't know that part." He shrugs. "I've gotta do it myself, you know?"

Do I know what it's like to feel responsible for someone else? "Yeah. I do know." I'm a big sister, after all.

He stares at me for a minute. "I'm talking a lot. What about you?" His voice softens. "I take it by your views on love that someone hurt you?"

Oh no way, buddy. I might be seeing things a bit differently, but that's not … no. My chest tightens at the thought of telling him about my family, even though he trusted me with information about his.

"Next question."

His pupils seem to vibrate in the dim light of the stateroom. "Okay." Then he reaches out and lightly touches my braid, which is lying on the bed between us. Picks it up, and flicks his thumb across the tip. "What's your natural color?"

Probably has no idea, but he couldn't have chosen a more personal question. "Next."

A hint of surprise colors his irises. "Favorite movie?"

Ah, this one I can answer. "*Iron Man*. The first one."

"I can definitely see that." Then he smiles.

And maybe it's my imagination, but his lips look a little less swollen. I reach out and ring my finger around the area to check. Then I freeze. Gah. What am I doing? *Cover it up! Say something!* "Um, your face looks better."

His eyebrows lift. "Feels better too."

"Good." A pause rents the air, a silence that shouts louder than a high school pep band. "Maybe we should, uh, go to sleep then?"

"Yeah. Sure." He has the good sense to yawn. "Whatever you say, RB."

I nod and dive to extinguish the light from my lamp, crawl under the covers in my clothes because I'm suddenly way too tired to change. Face the wall. Then a question itches its way in and it screams at me until I scratch it. "Why do you call me that?" I blurt.

"What?" His voice has taken on a sleepy quality, which perhaps means he's crashing from the adrenaline surge caused by the epinephrine. "RB?"

"Yeah. RB. Rainbow Brite. I always thought it was because of my hair, but then you said it wasn't."

"It's not."

I can tell he's drifting now, and my foot presses back, finds his again. I apply gentle pressure from my heel to the top of his foot. "Dax?"

"It's … your eyes. They light up." Silence. "Whenever we're"—yawn—"sparring. Never seen anything like it. Like all the colors of the rainbow in one single second."

Oh. Wow. Um. Resisting the urge to turn toward him, I keep my hands shoved underneath my pillow.

"It's beautiful," he mumbles. Then he's gone.

And so am I.

eleven

. . .

I NEVER THOUGHT I'd be here again.

When I read the cruise itinerary, saw we were going to St. Thomas, I didn't think I'd ever visited despite the many lavish vacations of my childhood. But the second I set foot on the Magens Bay beach, something inside me knew.

And broke.

Even though I didn't remember the name, I recognize it all. The outside bar and grill we passed several minutes ago in our search for an uninhabited portion of beach. The sailboats on the horizon. The lush vegetation just behind the sand, building up into a range of small hills enclosing the bay.

The white sand feels as familiar under my toes as breathing. Walking along the beach with Dax (who is back to his normal self after a good night of sleep) and the others, I have such an eerie sense of déjà vu that I nearly keel over. The past is pressing into me and I'm like a hollowed-out grotto vibrating, threatening to cave in.

There. That very spot under that very palm tree. Dad pulled a splinter out of my hand when I was eight.

That condo, with the yellow roof and pink walls. We stayed there. I'm sure of it. Inside is a small living room where we played endless rounds of Monopoly, where we curled up on the couch together and watched *Beauty and the Beast*, where Mom tried serving us burned popcorn and I dumped it out and my dad scolded me.

Where my dad promptly took me in his arms when I started crying at his harsh tone—because Daddy never raised his voice with me. I was his girl. His one and only.

Little did I know he had another on the way.

"Alexis?"

I stumble, halt, look up into Dax's eyes, which are covered with sunglasses. "Hmm?"

He waves to the rest of the group, urging them toward the spot Fred is leading us to—"It's the best spot on the beach, trust me!"—and pushes his shades to the top of his head. "What's wrong?"

I shake my head. No, I don't want to think about this. Not here. Not now.

Not ever, if I'm honest.

"I'm fine."

"The heck you are. You look like you've seen a ghost."

And for a minute, I see the apparition of a thirty-something man and a young girl playing in the calm water. I remember the warmth I didn't expect, the gentle undulation of the ocean that rocks and tilts but doesn't swirl or jolt.

Dax's hand on my upper arm dispels the vision. "I'm getting a little worried here, RB. Are you dehydrated or something? Spend too much time nursing me back to health last night?"

I quirk my lips. "Yeah, I did so much." Couldn't even bring myself to tell him one significant thing about myself. Meanwhile, he spilled his guts.

"Hey." His fingers trail down my arm, take my hand, squeeze. "You kept my mind off the aching in my stomach and head. That was okay in my book."

The Bennetts call to us, ask if we're okay. I squeeze his hand back, then pull away and hike up the beach bag strap on my shoulder. "You should go. I need to call my sister anyway. Told her I'd check in."

He hesitates. "If you're sure."

I nod and he trudges away, looking back at me a few times. My lungs let loose and I know exactly where my legs are carrying me before I can stop them. Plopping down in the sand, I lean back against the trunk of the tree where my dad always set up our blankets in the morning, before we were even ready to go out to the beach—"*So nobody snags the perfect spot from us, Lexi Bean.*"

And before I even have my sister on the video chat, I'm close to crying like a child. Somehow, the tears are held back. But they're closer than they've ever been to spilling over the edge.

Ugh. I do not want him to have this kind of power over me. No one should.

My sister's face pops on the screen. "Hey, girl! What's—Alexis? Are you okay? Did he hurt you? I'm going to come down there and, wait, where are you? It looks gorgeous."

"Focus, Kennedy." I pause. "I'm in St. Thomas, and I'm not upset because of Dax."

"That's both good and bad news, I suppose."

I squint and see a familiar blue behind her. "Where are *you*?"

"Oh. Um." She tilts her head, bites her lip. "Your house, actually."

"What?"

"Brooks and I had a fight and I just had to get away. I hope you don't mind. Shelby and Lauren have been super sweet."

"Of course I don't mind. Are you okay, though?" I sit up straighter, away from the tree. "Do you need me to come home? I can grab my bags off the ship and—"

"No, big sister. I'm fine. Just needed some space." She points at the screen. "But back to you."

"I'd rather talk about your problems."

"I'll bet you would."

I huff a strangled laugh. "Wait, what do you mean it's good and bad news I'm not crying over Dax?"

"Oh." Kennedy's hand flits through the air. "Well, good that he's not treating you like garbage, but bad that your time together hasn't made you finally confront all of your feelings over Dad and that piece-of-junk Corbin."

I blink at her, stunned at how perceptive she is at only twenty-three.

"Ooooh." She nods. "Maybe you *are* finally confronting your feelings."

"If I am, it's *not* because of Dax. I hate him."

Even I can tell that my voice lacks conviction. Her lips flatten and she murmurs something unintelligible.

"I'm upset because …" I look around again at this beautiful place. "We came here. For vacation. Me, Dad, and Mom. I didn't know what it was called, but it was definitely this bay."

"Oh, wow." Her voice goes soft. "You're so lucky you have some memories with him."

Lucky? "How can you say that? It's all tainted, Kennedy. This whole place. Every memory I have of him. I can't help but wonder what he was really thinking and feeling every time he was with us, because I can't trust that what he told me—what I remember— was true."

"You're such a black and white thinker." Kennedy sighs. "Alexis, did you ever consider that maybe Dad wasn't all good or all bad? That he could simultaneously love his life with you and also love his life with us? I mean, yeah, his methods weren't great and clearly he had issues, but from the things you've told me, the things my mom has told me, it sounds like he really loved both of us."

"But lying to someone isn't love."

"Lying and loving are two totally separate things. They don't really impact one another in my mind."

I swipe at a tear. "I don't get it."

"I don't know if I can really explain it." She screws up her face in that focused way she has. "Okay, like, lying isn't right. We know this." I wince at the matter-of-factness in her voice—because what have Dax and I been doing this whole week? Lying to the Bennetts. I can't think about that right now, though. I need to focus on whatever truth she's trying to impart. "But lying to someone also doesn't mean the loving wasn't real and true." She blows out a harsh breath. "Am I making any sense?"

"Strangely, yeah." But I still don't know how to reconcile it all.

"And as for Dax …"

I groan.

"Hear me out, sis. As for Dax, he's not all one thing either. No one is. Now, whether he's someone you want to get to know better or not, I have no clue since I've not met the man." Her eyes, now back to their natural cinnamon brown, bore into me. "Ever since Corbin—but let's be honest, even before that—you form opinions about people, and rarely do you allow that opinion to change. But what if you let yourself see Dax differently than just your workplace enemy? At the very least, maybe he could be a friend."

A friend. Yeah. Maybe. "To be honest, Ken, I've already started to see that there's more than I knew." Because even though Dax has been lying right along with me, I can sense there's maybe something different about him. Or maybe I just am starting to want to believe that.

Regardless, I wince at the admission.

"Aha! See? I'm right. For that, I'm stealing some of your ice cream from the freezer tonight."

I chuckle. "Don't pretend you haven't already done that."

"Fine. Guilty." Then Kennedy brings the phone even closer to her face so I can see her—really see her. "Alexis Matkin, you have this huge capacity to love. I mean, look at me. You could have seen me as one thing—an enemy—but you chose differently. And you can choose this too."

I bring my knees to my chest. "I don't know how to be different, Kennedy. All I see when I start to try is Dad's face. Corbin and that woman together. Betrayal is hard to get past. Just like this place, it colors everything."

"I know, sis. Maybe just start small, even if it's hard. You don't have to open yourself up all at once. This isn't a sprint. It's a marathon."

"I hate running."

"Me too. It's a sisterly bond we share."

I laugh. "Thanks, Ken. I'm going to try."

"There is no try. Just do!"

"Ugh, you sound like those stupid motivational posters Nate has plastered around the office."

"Well, I *was* a cheerleader in high school." She raises a pretend pom-pom in the air. "Alexis, Alexis, she's our gal! If she can't open up and be vulnerable and find love again, er … no one shall!"

"You're ridiculous and I love you." I smile through the tears.

"Same, girl. Same." Then my sister blows me a kiss, says goodbye, and hangs up.

Lowering the phone, I sit there for a bit, considering

her words. Is it possible to be different? What if … what if I could notice the beauty in a place that's left a wound? Can new memories be formed here? Can I erase the dark colors I've given the pictures of my family and me, add brightness back to them?

And if I can do that, maybe I could also choose to trust another man. Not even in the romantic sense, but as a friend, like Kennedy suggested. It's actually crazy to think I've not had a male friend since Corbin cheated on me. Even my friends' husbands and fiancés, I keep at arms' length. I've never really bothered to get to know them well, because deep down I wonder if they're honestly any different than the men in my experience.

I mean, I chose Corbin because he was safe. He wasn't the most attractive guy in the room with his slight dad bod and glasses, curly hair that never seemed quite under control. Though I loved how smart he was, how kind he was—he worked at a pet shelter, for crying out loud!—I wasn't even all that attracted to him in an explosive way. More like a steady way.

Because *he* was steady. Steady job. Steady routine. Steady kisses. Predictable. And I liked that.

The one thing that I didn't predict? The fling with one of his volunteers. And that's when I knew—even the steady guys abandon ship at some point.

But that's me. When did I become this person who doesn't even truly believe her *best friends* have found happiness? I mean, I wish it for them—of course I do. But there's a part of me that doesn't actually know if a guy is capable of real, true, honest love.

As I stare out at tourists frolicking in the waves,

soaking up the sun and rays in this beautiful place, I realize just how messed up that is.

I gather my things, stand to my wobbling feet, and start down the beach. In the distance, the Bennetts are spread out on blankets and Gloria and Landon stand in the bay, holding each other in peaceful water that's spread out like thin jam on toast. The sky is clear of clouds and stretches as blue and lovely as the bay. Their joy and peace are evident even from here.

And then there's Dax. He's leaning against a tree, hands in his pockets, and he's looking down the beach in my direction.

Almost as if he's waiting for me.

twelve

"WAIT, WHAT DID YOU SAY?" I blink at Fred, who stands near the excursions desk where Dax and I are waiting for our group to embark on a snorkel and catamaran excursion in Barbados.

Well, I thought the whole group was going. But Fred has just blown that assumption wide open.

"We thought you could use a little time away from the old people." He nudges Dax with his elbow, a wide grin on his very-pleased-with-himself face. "Of course, Gloria couldn't do anything overly adventurous due to her condition, so we booked them a nice relaxing couples massage."

Oh, thank goodness they didn't do that for us. Don't you just wear towels for those? Not that I've ever had one but … yeah. I'm sweaty just thinking about it. I glance at Dax out of the corner of my eye. Our gazes meet and he waggles his eyebrows a bit, but I don't detect any indication that he knew about this change in plans.

Honestly, it should be a relief. Playacting for the last week since we embarked has started to wear on me. Gloria is still watching me with the vigilance of a meerkat, which means I'm constantly aware of the need to be holding Dax's hand or staring lovingly at him or slipping my arm around his very solid waist.

There hasn't been any more kissing, though. We haven't actually talked about that boundary, but he hasn't initiated one and neither have I—even if my dreams have relived the first incident a few times.

What? It was a good kiss. Objectively speaking. It has nothing to do with Dax himself.

Yeah, even I don't believe myself anymore.

Speaking of Dax, I've taken Kennedy's advice. Started to open up, just a little to him, as a friend. Completely platonic friends who are pretending to be engaged in front of an audience and maybe play footsie on the bed, but THAT'S IT. I've managed to wrangle my traitorous body into submission even though it's been urging me to do something drastic like curl up against him while we watch movies at night (trading off between rom-coms and superhero movies, of course).

Do I want to really test that resolve with a whole day where it's just him and me?

Not really.

Do I have a choice? Doesn't look like it.

He must sense my hesitancy—or maybe he has some himself—because Dax runs a hand through his hair, something I'm learning is a nervous tic of his. "That's really generous of you guys. But are you sure you don't want to come along? This excursion looks really awesome."

He's right. We'll board a catamaran and then go snorkeling in two different locations, one that boasts a ton of sea turtles, then have drinks as we cruise back. From what I've seen, the weather is perfect, thus my clothing choice of my bikini, shorts, T-shirt, and flip-flops.

"No, no, the ladies have a hankering for some shopping, so that's our plan for today."

"Didn't get enough of that the last few days?" I tease.

"Who are you kidding? Janet and Cecilia could out shop Betty Halbreich herself."

From what I saw of them the last two days as we explored St. Lucia and Antigua together, that's totally accurate. We all laugh and then Fred leaves us with the excursion group, which is mostly assembled.

Dax pulls his sunglasses off his head and leans back against the decorative wall in the lobby where we're waiting. The smooth European marble flooring spreads out like a puddle around us. It looks so different in the daytime, illuminated by the sun shining through the glass roof instead of by fake lights. "You okay with this? If you want to go hide out in the room, I'll get out of your hair and go on the trip without you."

Huh. He's being surprisingly insightful. And sweet. I shrug. "I think the fresh air will be good for me."

"Because there's been such a lack of it lately."

He has a point since we've been outside almost

exclusively the last week, but I stick my tongue out at him. "I just really want to snorkel, okay? I've never been." I was too scared as a kid, and then my mom and I never took another vacation together after my dad died. She does that with her new husband now.

His eyebrows shoot up. "Round of Never Have I Ever?"

This is our new thing the last few days—playing stupid get-to-know-you games. It started on St. Thomas, after my talk with Kennedy.

I was still feeling shaky, but rejoined the group, and their joy drew me in. We all floated in the bay, the waters so calm I could just sluice my arms through it and swim like it was a pool. And when I got out and sat on my towel, Dax joined me on his.

Then he surprised me. "You up for a round of My Favorite Things?"

I arched an eyebrow at him, considered his request in light of what Kennedy had said about offering him friendship. Chewed my bottom lip. Made him wait a while before answering. "Why?"

"I just don't know much about you except work stuff. Guess I thought it would help. You know, with this whole charade."

Oh. Right. "Okay. Nothing crazy, though. I'm not telling you my deepest, darkest secrets."

"So no asking what made you upset earlier?"

I pursed my lips, shook my head. "That wouldn't be one of my favorite things anyway."

"Got it. Right." A pause. "Favorite color."

"Lime green. You?"

"Red." Another pause. "Like that red your hair was the first time we met. Not super bright and orangey, but not deep red either. It was just right. I don't know that I've ever seen the color before or since. It was … inspired."

The sand seemed to shift beneath me and I smoothed my hand over my towel. Cheeks warm, I continued the game. "Favorite candy."

"Snickers, because I like to laugh."

That made me snort. "How about the taste?"

"You can't go wrong with chocolate of any sort."

"Hey, look. We actually agree on something." I shot him a wry grin.

That game turned into a version of 20 Questions where we just asked random questions of each other, not necessarily favorites. I learned he likes to go hiking, that he isn't really a sports-watching kind of guy, that his childhood dream was to be one of Santa's elves, that he's an only child, and that his cousin Joe is his ride or die.

When the twenty questions were asked and answered, I grabbed a fistful of sand and let it filter from my palm. "Dax?"

"Yeah, RB?"

"This changes nothing," I whispered. "I still loathe you as much as ever."

"I know." His voice cradled a smile in it, and that made me smile too.

In addition to those games, so far we've also played Two Truths and a Lie—which Dax is surprisingly bad at —and had a full conversation entirely in movie quotes.

That one was hilarious, since most of his were from classic rom-coms and most of mine from Marvel movies.

"Okay." I nod.

But at that moment, the excursion director calls us together, gives us the basic rules, then leads us off the boat, and out onto a catamaran. The next hour and a half are fairly magical, with the sun and the sea and … well, the company. When we aren't competing for the same clients, when I'm not viewing him as someone to merely tolerate, when I do my best to forget that he's a hot specimen of a man and think of him in friendly terms, I actually kind of like being with him. Don't mind it, anyway.

And here, as we play our silly game, then slip on face masks and flippers, jump from the ladder into the warm water, swim around the cove and point out bright fish and turtles that spark my creativity and make me itch to draw something, there's no pressure.

We just … are.

A few hours later, as we settle ourselves onto a huge thick-roped net strung along the back of the catamaran for the ride back to land, I'm more comfortable with Dax than I have ever felt. It helps that we just shared an amazing experience and I'm riding the high of that.

It also helps that I have rum punch in my hands and haven't had to perpetuate a fraud to anyone all day.

Dax seems to agree. Sighing, he stretches out and lays his head back against the portion of netting that slopes upward. "I really needed today." His white linen shirt is unbuttoned and his skin has definitely grown even tanner than before thanks to all the sun this week.

I do my best not to ogle him, but am fairly sure he's noticed my not-so-discreet glances his way. "What do you mean?" A sip of the punch showcases its flavor as tart and fruity at the same time. Just the way I like it.

"Don't you think it's been an exhausting week? Having to be *on* all the time?"

"I get that." Droplets of sea spray mist over the back of the boat as we speed up. "Personally, I'd choose you over Landon any day. That guy has no personality."

He sits up slightly. "Hold up. *You'd* pick *me*? Miracles do happen."

"Don't go getting too excited there, Booger Bear." I smirk. "I would also pick my garbage man with the sock fetish and the cashier at my grocery store who always wants to talk about the latest naughty novel she's reading over Landon, so … yeah."

"I see where I rate." He nudges me with his elbow and settles back, his arm slung behind his head. "I don't know, though. I think they really like that Landon and Gloria are already married with kids." He looks sideways at me, swirls his drink. "Tom asked me the other day why we haven't set a wedding date. Apparently Cecilia is worried about us."

"Oh." The icky feeling that has come with our charade is something I've tried to shove to the back of my mind, because most of the time I don't feel like I'm lying to the Bennetts—just that we're hanging out, talking about our favorite places to eat or books and movies we enjoy. It feels like they're friends.

Except for when they ask for details about my relationship with Dax. I try to change the subject as best I can, but there are times when questions inevitably have to be answered. "Yeah, the women keep trying to ask me personal questions too." My cheeks warm at the memory of something they asked this morning.

"Like what?"

I cough. "Uh …"

"Ooo, sounds juicy."

"It could be."

"Come on, RB, don't leave me hanging."

Fine, he wants to know? "Like about the physical side of our relationship. Those fifty-somethings want to hear all the dirty details. They're surprisingly, um, feisty."

His eyes widen as he sucks down a sip, choking on his punch and coughing into his sleeve. When he's recovered, he asks, "What do you tell them?"

"Wouldn't you like to know?" I say this in a rumbly, sultry voice filled with teasing.

Dax fiddles with a button on his shirt. "Well, we *should* probably get our stories straight."

I smack him in the chest. "Dax, what do you think, that I'd make up erotic stories about us just to satisfy their curiosity?"

"Well …" He grins at me, and goofball Dax is back. "After how much you enjoyed that kiss the other night—"

My harrumph is so loud that another couple stops their conversation and eyes us. But I ignore them and fix Dax with laser eyes. "I was just playing a part, remember?"

"So you didn't enjoy it?"

"I ... that's not what ... argh."

He laughs, seemingly as carefree as the boat careening along the shoreline. "If it helps, I always enjoy kissing a gorgeous woman."

My drink burns going down. "I suppose I should be grateful to be one of so many." I try for a tease but my tone comes out grumpy instead.

Because the thought of Dax kissing other women is strangely grating.

Dax groans. "Alexis, that's not ... I just meant to say, you are." His foot bumps mine. "You're gorgeous."

Oh. No, no, no. Uh uh, sir.

He can't be saying stuff like this. It's making me feel things ... things I don't want to feel. Not just a physical reaction but a fondness that goes beyond friendship. My body is going to overthrow my heart and the coup will not end well. Much blood will be spilled. "Yeah, well, you're gorgeous too. So? That's why we're a good match. For this business deal, I mean."

Yes, good. Remind him—both of us—that we are here for one reason and one reason only. To get him that job. And maybe to become friends. But that's totally secondary.

We're both quiet for a bit. Then, "You think I'm gorgeous, you want to kiss me ..." And now he's quoting lines from *Miss Congeniality* in the most ridiculous voice and I'm groaning and rolling my eyes.

And thank the stars, the tension is broken. We chat about a few other things, laugh about something the Bennetts told us at breakfast. Then, I grow more serious. "Doesn't it bother you? The lying? They're such nice people."

"I know." He blows out a hard breath. "It's killing me, to be honest."

I tilt my head back and look at him. "Really?"

"Yeah."

"Me too." My teeth find my bottom lip. "There are so many kinds of lies, you know? White lies we tell others or ourselves to smooth things over or avoid something awkward. Lies that protect others. Lies that are malicious and intentionally harmful. Lies that are borne out of desperation." Like with my dad, maybe. Wow, I'm rambling. "Sorry. I guess I've just been thinking a lot lately about lying—about whether it's ever okay."

"Don't be sorry." A pause. "So, any conclusions? *Is* it ever okay?"

"Still pondering *that* mystery of the universe." My lips quirk momentarily. "But honestly, I think that when it comes down to it, it doesn't matter the motivation. Lies will always put a wedge between people. Sometimes small, sometimes big, but even the small ones have the potential to grow and do harm."

He's quiet for several long minutes. Another couple gets up and walks inside the boat, their movement jostling the rope beneath us as I wait, my nerves humming. How will Dax respond to this glimpse inside Alexis? I know I've not been overly personal with what I just shared—no gritty details of my past or even present—but it's a tiny sliver of my heart nonetheless. Will he take that sliver and cherish it for what it is, or completely berate me and call me a hypocrite (which I probably deserve because I've been lying too)?

Finally, I get my answer.

"When we started this whole thing, I was just desperate," he says, his voice so low and husky that I have to lean closer to hear it over the boat's motor. "And it didn't seem like pretending would hurt anyone. But now I see the way they've really become attached to us, so involved in our lives ..."

"They have a way of doing that, don't they?" Honestly, Janet and Cecilia have been more mothering toward me than my own mom has ever been—at least since Dad died. They've given advice and listened and just generally accepted me, flaws and all. "The thought of never seeing them again after this ..."

Because I won't, whether Dax gets the job or not. He might go on being in a relationship with them, but he'll have to tell them we broke up. I will become the non-entity in all of this, and that makes the rum punch curdle in my stomach.

"Dang," he says. "I hadn't even thought of that."

How could he not?

He downs the rest of his drink, exposing the underside of his chin for a second. I'm drawn to the stubble along his jawline, his neck, his Adam's apple. "Guess I've been trying to shove down thoughts of *what if*, you know? Live in the moment. Enjoy this time with them." Then he spears me with a look. "This time with you."

There's no glimmer of amusement or teasing in his eyes when he says that. Which makes me think … well, I don't have the bandwidth to admit it to myself. I force a chuckle. "It beats work, that's for sure."

He doesn't smile back, just studies me like I'm an onion he wants to peel. "I'm serious, Alexis. This trip has been nothing like I thought it'd be."

"What—" *Do not ask him what he means. Do not!* Gah. "Um, me either."

"What did you think it would be? In fact"—he taps his foot against mine—"why did you really come on this trip, Alexis? I mean, I know you want to get rid of me, but why is that so important to you?"

What a question. "You mean other than my general loathing of you?"

The boat turns and my body rocks sideways, pushing my arm against Dax's. And there's no reason I have to stay there when we straighten—nobody's watching us, after all. But I do.

He chuckles. "Sure." Clearly he doesn't believe me. And who can blame him?

Ugh, *fine.* "My friends are all moving out once they get married next year."

He's clearly not satisfied with this answer, because he just waits, eyebrows lifted.

I toss back my cup, but it's empty. "If you leave and I get your accounts, I'll be able to pay off the rest of what I owe on my mortgage so I don't need to take on more housemates."

"Okay." His silence seems to ask me why that's important.

Sighing, I nearly pout at Kennedy's voice in my head, telling me to play nice, to share myself with him. "You might have figured out that it's hard for me to make friends."

His face breaks into an adorable grin I want to smack off—and also kiss.

Whoa! Uh uh. Bad Alexis. Where did that thought come from? The Kiwi Kiss of Death was the only mouth-to-mouth I'll be giving Dax Nyhart. (Unfortunately. What? Gah!)

As if he can hear my thoughts, Dax grins wider.

I suppress a shiver and go on. "So I would rather live on my own."

"Oh come on, Alexis. There has to be more to it than that. You went on a cruise with your mortal enemy, after all. That's desperation if I ever heard it."

"Hey! Maybe I really *am* just that desperate to get rid of you."

"Sure, sure. What about your sister?"

"What about her?"

"Didn't you say she was in California? Couldn't she move in with you and help with the bills?"

"She lives in San Francisco with her boyfriend. Although I just found out there's trouble in paradise. But I could never depend on her for money." At the question in his eyes, I continue. "Okay, the other reason I want to pay off my house is so she has the option to come live with me without feeling like she has to pay me rent. I'd also like to provide her with a place to stay in case she wants to go back to school. Maybe pay for her tuition too."

"Can't she get a loan?"

"Probably, but loans set you on a really bad track in life. And my sister … well, she's just not good with money. It would not be a good thing for her to owe the government massive sums." Even though he hasn't made a negative comment, I feel suddenly defensive of her. "She hasn't ever worked a regular job. She's lived off of a trust fund inheritance for years—and that's nearly gone—and uses what little she makes as a social media influencer on expensive dinners out with her boyfriend."

"Who, judging by your tone, you obviously don't approve of."

My grip tightens on my cup, making the plastic creak. "Don't get me started."

"Ooo, someone else has earned your ire. This I have to hear."

I smile, roll my eyes. "Don't worry, Booger Bear. You'll always be at the top of my list."

"Will I really, RB?" His eyebrows lift and there's something about the way he looks at me then, something that makes me want to shrink away, plop through one of the tiny squares in the netting and disappear right out to sea.

The look is there and gone in seconds, though.

"Of course you will." I lift the cup to my lips again before remembering it has nothing in it. My eyes whip toward the boat's employee—Elvis—walking bowlegged along the net, offering drink refills.

As I hold up my drink, he smiles at me. "Here ya go, pretty lady." Winks as he pours some more punch into first my cup, then Dax's. A little splashes down onto my bare legs.

"Thanks, Elvis. You're my new best friend."

His grin widens, teeth burning all the whiter because of his richly dark skin. "And you're mine, pretty lady," he says before moving on to the next couple.

Dax chuckles. "Looks like I've got some competition."

"Ply me with drinks and I become putty in your hands."

"Is that what it takes, then? Hmm." He chuckles, then sobers. "But back to your sister. RB … it sounds like you're going to great lengths to take care of someone who is old enough to take care of herself." His voice is gentle, but still stabbing in its accuracy.

"I know that. But she had a rough childhood." Pippa was a decent mom, but she was caught up in the Hollywood lifestyle, bouncing among various rich producer boyfriends until moving them to San Diego a year before she died. That's when Kennedy moved to San Francisco for college and started her partying lifestyle. Dropped out of college. Met Brooks. "I just want to be that steadying influence for her, you know?"

Wait. Of course he knows. "What you said earlier about going to great lengths—don't you think you're doing that with your mom?"

His mouth opens, closes, no sound sneaking out. Then, "Well—"

"I mean, you're here too, pretending to be engaged

of all things, just so you can have the chance at paying off her house. And all the stuff you did as a kid, growing up. You had to sacrifice a lot."

He shrugs. "Not really."

"Tell me one thing you had to give up. Something that mattered to you, that you sacrificed because of your mom's disease. Because you were the one working your butt off like an adult even though you were just a teenager." I don't know where this righteous anger is coming from. Maybe it was boiling under the surface all along.

"I did those things willingly. She didn't make me."

"That doesn't mean you didn't sacrifice. And it definitely doesn't mean you should have had to."

"I can't think of any—"

"Dax Nyhart, don't you lie to me."

That phrasing seems to affect him, probably because of our earlier conversation. His jaw clenches and his eyes flicker. "Swimming."

I wait. Then, "Go on."

He sighs. "I loved swim team. Started when I was just six, back when Dad was still there. I swam club for years, till Mom's addiction got really bad. We couldn't afford that anymore so I just swam on the school team, till I got too busy with work. I even had a college scout interested ..."

His tone has gone from uptight to sad, a bit broken, almost as if he's just discovering that this isn't normal. Like he's still fighting the realization, he says, "But I'm her son."

"That doesn't mean you should have to bear all the

weight in your relationship." I hold up a hand. "And before you say I should talk, I recognize that some of my tendencies toward Kennedy are not healthy either. Maybe I'll have to work on that. Thankfully, our relationship isn't fully one-sided. She supports me in other ways." Like our conversation in St. Thomas.

"Huh." He shakes his head. "You amaze me. You just blurt out these tiny bits of wisdom as if they're nothing. And you have this way of making me see things differently." Dax studies me. "I like that. And I'll miss it when I'm gone."

Oh. My. Stars. Maybe he means it in a friendly-you-challenge-me-like-a-good-colleague-would way, but sheesh. The way my insides are melting, you'd think he'd just told me he loves me or some other such nonsense.

I've GOT to get back to teasing. It's my only recourse at this point. "Sooooo confident you're going to get this job, huh?" I poke him in the side.

"Why wouldn't I?" He grabs my finger. "Wait, don't answer that."

"Ooo, tempting." Trying to pull my hand back, I laugh as he won't let go, continuing to sip on his drink as if he's not holding my finger hostage. "You'd better get it. Otherwise, I'm still stuck with you." I give my finger another little tug and he releases it. Instantly, I kind of regret not keeping it there.

Which is silly. Because I'm trying to be Dax's friend. I'm not ready for more than that. I mean, if I *were* to choose a guy to let into my life *in that way*, maybe it would be him. But it doesn't do any good to think like that. I'm completely screwed up and I just don't know if I can get there.

What I *do* know? The thought of Dax leaving makes me want to crawl onto his lap, hug him tight, and not let go. But this trip just might be some magical bubble that has no bearing on reality. Once we leave here, who will we be?

"But really, it will all work out how it's supposed to," I manage.

"Ah. Believer in fate, are we?"

"No. In making your own way. You're smart. You're good at what you do. And you're a hard worker." And freaking sweet to be doing it all just so he can make more money to take care of his mom—who, he confided in me earlier, was a bit nervous for him to be on this trip; he had to make sure she had all the information to reach him in case she felt she needed him.

But I don't say this because I don't want him knowing I think he's sweet—even if I do. "You'll find your way."

"Hold up. Did *the* Alexis Matkin just give me not one, not two, but three compliments?"

I down my drink to hide my smile. "All this sun has addled my brain. I don't know who I am anymore." Ain't that the truth?

"Whoever you are, I kinda like you this way."

I feel the blush rising in my cheeks again and slosh my cup around, taking some ice between my teeth. "That's just because we're on the same team for once."

"But we make a pretty good team, don't we?" Another elbow nudge and I suddenly get the itch to lean my head against his shoulder, to grab his hand—things I've been doing a lot this week, so I should be sick of it. But there's no one around to see it, so I can't justify it or play it off as part of the charade.

And the worst thing in the world would be for Dax to think I'm falling for him, especially if he fully still sees this as merely a business transaction.

It's a really good thing I'm *not* falling for him. That would be embarrassing. Who falls for their enemy, anyway?

thirteen

. . .

A FEW HOURS LATER, I study myself in the full-length mirror attached to the wall across from the bed. Tuck, pull, smooth.

Breathe.

The delicate spaghetti straps of the dress I wore to Evie's wedding run the same course as my bikini top, so thankfully my new tan lines aren't ruining the effect. The deep burgundy isn't a color I'd have chosen on my own, but I suppose with my blue hair, there's kind of a cool dark-and-bright contrast going on.

I do rather like the style of the dress. It's comfortable —with pockets, hello!—gathering at the waist and flaring out to the hem, under which I'm wearing silver-heeled sandals. The sweetheart neckline still leaves much to the imagination, but emphasizes my exceptional clavicle. Given the crisscrossing straps in back, one of the best features of the dress is the built-in bra. Did I mention the dress was comfortable?

Leaning forward, I pick up my lipstick tube and dab on a layer of New York Red. There. With my hair swinging free—the first time this whole trip it's been in anything but a braid—I feel sexy and powerful.

And still me.

It's funny. I was appalled at Kayla's clothing choices at first, but once I busted out of my routine—out of my comfort zone, like she suggested—I realized I could feel okay in anything she gave me because she actually chose well. Guess she knows me better than I thought.

"Whoa."

The word behind me is nearly inaudible, but I hear it all the same. Glancing up in the mirror, I find Dax standing beside the bed in a suit. He's blinking and rubbing his chin and staring. At me.

He approaches and I feel every one of my nerve endings as they catch the spark coming from his gaze. Then he hooks me in a hug, my back to his chest, his arms around my shoulders and clasped in front of me. We look at each other through the mirror.

"I've been thinking about what you said," he says, setting his chin against my temple. "And I'm going to tell them the truth."

My heart stalls. "The Bennetts?"

A nod. "I was so desperate to provide for my mom, but that's no excuse for lying, is it?" Dax's breath tickles my face. "I think you're right about it driving a wedge in relationships. I really want that job, but how can I honestly work with those guys, have them invest in me like I know they would, and not ever tell them the truth? It would always be between us. Better to come clean now, even if it means sacrificing the job."

"Wow." That's all I can say, because this level of honesty and integrity? To admit when he's wrong, to do what we both know is the right thing no matter what it will cost him?

I never expected it, especially from a man. Left and right, Dax Nyhart is just blowing all of my expectations about men out of the water.

I have to test this, to make sure it's real. "Are you sure?"

"Yes. Because anything worth having should be founded in truth, don't you think?" His look sears me straight through the mirror—and I'm wondering what exactly he's asking me. If he's just talking about the job now.

He is, right? He has to be.

And yet, my breath gets stuck in my throat as I swallow. Because practically, what does this mean for the rest of our trip? "When are you going to tell them?" *When will the charade be up?*

"Soon. I don't want to ruin a nice evening or the rest of the trip for anyone but … yeah. Soon. I promise."

Nothing is as attractive to me as an honest man. Oh, goodness. I *am* falling for him, aren't I?

So what if you are? Maybe there's a happy ending for you after all, if he's not moving to LA. If you can take your time, really get to know him …

I mean, I knew Corbin too. But being in *his* arms never felt like this.

Clearing my throat, I bite the inside of my cheek. "What will you do then? Ask Nate for a raise?"

"I've seen the books. He can't afford it." His arms squeeze around me, tighter until my skin feels like it's branded. "I've got another job offer."

"Wait, really? Since when?"

"It's kind of a standing offer from a college buddy. I wanted the Bennett Toys job because I'd still be close to Mom. I know she's been clean for a good while, but I still can't help but feel like she needs me."

"She's an adult, Dax. You're not responsible for her sobriety."

"Yeah, I know. But just like you want to be there for Kennedy, I still want to do what I can for Mom."

And that's why I like this guy. Ugh. Noooo. "So, this other job is a good one too?"

"Yeah."

There's something he isn't saying. "Where is it?" My voice is froggy, hoarse.

And his eyes are hooded, shadowed. "Texas." The word is a whispered curse.

My body goes numb at this news. So he's leaving either way. Okay, then. *Buck up, Alexis. He's just going to be a friend after all.*

Licking my lips, I turn into him, step back, adjust his tie like the future married couple we're pretending to be. Sometimes, it all feels real. A little too real. And yet, in this moment, I have no wish for true reality to take over. Pretending feels too … electric. Amazingly so.

And if it's all ending soon, I'm going to ride this feeling to the end of the line.

"You clean up nice, Booger Bear." I pat his blue tie, run my thumb down its smooth surface.

"Look who's talking, Rainbow Brite. You're glowing."

Oh, stars.

A tingle turns into a full-on shiver when he pulls a section of my hair from behind my shoulder, letting it drop in front. Dax rubs it between his forefinger and thumb. "I don't think I've ever seen your hair down."

"What? No. Really?"

"Really." He swallows. "I'd have remembered."

My hands slide from Dax's tie down his chest to his hips, landing just inside his jacket, resting on the top of his belt. I blink, take a small step in reverse, but he comes with me, and my back is now against the mirror. He's leaning with one forearm perched above me, his other still touching my hair. His fingers move up, up, along the strands until they're in my roots, cradling the base of my head. The cinnamon-tinted citrus of his cologne engulfs me, and suddenly I don't think there's anything sexier than a man in a suit.

We are leaning and blinking and now his nose is pressed into my hair and I'm closing my eyes, inhaling him, my heart pounding with a question, begging for an answer.

What. Is. Happening?

I can't … no. He's leaving.

A forced laugh falls from my lips. "Guess we should be getting to dinner, huh?"

"What?" His voice is uneven, slightly broken. "Oh." Dax pulls back, straightens his tie. "Yeah. You're right."

My breath comes a little more steadily. "Awesome!" Aaaaand I definitely just sounded like a thirteen-year-old cheerleader. "Let's go."

Dax chuckles, and it might be a little tight, but all is right with the world. I snatch my little clutch and we head out the door and to the formal dining room, where the Bennetts are also dressed to the nines in floor-length gowns and tuxedos. Gloria and Landon show up a minute later, Landon typing something into his phone—does he actually have service?—before sliding it into his pocket and giving Tom and Fred both a hearty handshake.

All through dinner, the conversation is lively and we laugh a lot. Landon tells sweeping stories about his childhood on a farm as one of twelve children, and I see Tom and Fred exchange a look of appreciation—maybe over the fact that Landon has such a strong family background. Would that seriously sway their decision?

And even though I know Dax is going to tell them the truth, which will probably disqualify him from the job anyway, I do not like the idea of anyone thinking less of Dax simply because of a background he can't control. None of us should be judged by our parents' actions.

Before I know what I'm doing, I take Dax's arm and sling it across my shoulders. His fingers start to play with my dress strap, a move that drives me a tiny bit wild. But I manage to focus enough to ask, "Are you and the rest of your family still close, Landon?"

"Well." He takes a bite of his steak, chews. "They

live in the Midwest, so it's hard to get together more than on the holidays."

"Plus he's very committed to his job." Gloria moves her food around on her plate, nudging the green beans into her mashed potatoes. "And his immediate family. Kids take up a lot of time, as you'll find out when you two eventually get married."

Eventually. Was that a dig because we haven't set a wedding date yet? "Of course they do. And Dax is going to make a great dad someday." I casually spread butter across my roll, the gleam of the light fixture above us glinting off my knife. "You know, one of the things I love best about him is his commitment to his mother."

"Is that right?" Fred leans forward, elbows on the table.

"Yes. He's over there every weekend fixing things up for her—she's got some health issues, has since he was younger and he had to work three jobs just to keep them afloat. He even quit swim team and gave up the chance at a college scholarship." I keep my eyes on Gloria as I take a bite of my roll. *Take that, Gloria.*

Gloria forks a green bean. Hard. "Landon gets up in the middle of the night and changes Sammy's dirty diapers when I'm too tired."

"Isn't that just his job as a father?" I draw lazy circles in the condensation of my water, like I'm bored. "Dax works sixty-hour weeks so his mom can stay in the same house she's comfortable in."

"Landon makes it a point to take me on a date every other week."

"Dax takes me on a date *every* week."

"Landon gives me foot rubs while I'm pregnant."

"Dax gives me foot rubs when I'm not."

Our volleys have escalated in volume, and I notice Dax's fingers digging into my shoulder. It's not a pleasant sensation. I stop talking, realize my heart is running away, pounding so hard I can feel the chains, the bricks, rumbling around inside me.

Realize that everyone at the table is staring at me. Okay, so that didn't go exactly as I planned it.

I reach for another roll. "So, how about them Padres?"

Lucky for me, the Padres had a fantastic season this year, so my game of verbal volleyball with Gloria is forgotten. At least, I think it is, until dinner is over and Dax pulls me into the hallway while we wait for the rest of the ladies to use the restroom before moving on to our next activities.

"That was some performance in there." His drawn brow, flat lips, are not the usual fare for him.

My eyebrows knit together. "Oh, you mean how I defended you? Didn't you see how Fred and Tom were being all appreciative of Landon's bragging regarding the fact he grew up with a dozen siblings? It's not your fault you're an only child. I just wanted to even the playing field." I pause. "Are you upset?"

"No. But you don't have to do that anymore, remember? I'm going to tell them the truth. I've already made peace with Landon getting the job."

"You're right. I got carried away." I tilt my head. "Is that all that's wrong?"

"Nothing's wrong." He kicks at the floor. "It's just …"

"Just?" I roll my hand in the air in the universal let's-get-on-with-it motion.

"It was nice to hear the affection in your voice. To know you don't see me as the enemy anymore. Even if it's all for show." He glances up at me, then behind me. Before I can respond—not that I really know how—he leans in and gives me a quick kiss on the cheek. "I'm going gambling with the guys. I'll be back late."

As he joins Fred and Tom a few feet away, I press my hand against the spot he kissed. What was that all about?

"I think I was wrong about you two."

Ah. He saw Gloria coming. I'm not the only one "performing." Funny thing? For me, it wasn't actually a performance. It just felt natural to stick up for him, to be on his team.

If only Past Alexis could see me now …

I shake my head, drop my hand. "What do you mean?"

She smirks and Gloria's hand obnoxiously finds her stomach, again. Her long locks are pulled back into an elegant bun at the nape of her neck, and her eyes are actually soft right now. What's up with that? "Sorry I got a little carried away at dinner. Landon just really wants this job, you know?"

"I know." I cross my arms, wariness creeping into my chest. "What did you mean about being wrong?"

"I'm just remembering how presumptuous I was at the beginning of the trip—you know, when I said that you seemed tense around Dax." She smiles, tucks a wayward strand of hair back into her bun. "I can see now, with the way you defended him, that you really love him. And it's no secret to anyone with eyes how much he loves you."

Whaaaaat? "Um." I smooth my hands down my skirt. "What do you mean? H-how can you tell?" *Why are you asking this, Alexis? You do not care. He's. Leaving.*

"Just the way he looks at you. You know. Like he's a golden retriever and you're a piece of cheese."

Wait, huh? Do dogs even like cheese? "So, like he wants to devour me?"

Her tittering laugh joins the piano music keying up from the main lobby down the hall. "You're so funny, Alexis. I've really liked getting to know you." She places a hand on my arm. Squeezes. "And I really am sorry about that night when I pried into your relationship. It's just … well, my sister was in an emotionally abusive relationship, so I'm always on the lookout for red flags. But"—she rushes on—"I was definitely wrong in your case. Please, can you forgive me?"

Shoot. "That's terrible." My mind turns over to Kennedy. Brooks is bad enough, and to my knowledge he's just selfish, not abusive. But if he'd ever hurt her like that, I'm sure I'd read into situations in the same way Gloria did.

I'd also key his truck—or worse—but that's beside the point.

"I'm so sorry," I continue. "Is your sister okay?"

"She is now, after lots of therapy. Thank you for asking." She pulls me into a hug. "You're a sweet soul,

Alexis. I hope that, no matter which of our men gets the job, we can stay friends after this."

Okay, the guilt is coming hard and fast now. Like, really hard. It's pummeling me, in waves. "I'd like that." But will she ever be able to forgive me, once she finds out I'm not who I say I am? Will the Bennetts?

Ugh. Yuck. This feels … not good. Lying to people I genuinely like.

And suddenly, I'm wondering—is this how my dad felt? How Corbin felt, if he ever really cared about me like he claimed? Is Kennedy right that people can make bad decisions and still love someone genuinely?

A memory hits sudden. Fast. One I'd buried so deep I've just now found it again.

I was nine or so, and my dad had just gotten back from a cross-country trip. He knocked on my door. I was reading in bed, and when I saw it was him, I squealed. Jumped up and swung into his arms like I was five again. "You're back, you're back, you're back."

"Aw, Lexi Bug. I missed you like crazy, kid." He squeezed me so tight I thought I might explode from happiness. The times he came back were always the best. Mom was so sad when he was gone, and when he returned we always had a fun day out. They'd pull me out of school or we'd go for ice cream or to the zoo. Something to celebrate the fact our family was whole again.

Then he tucked me in. "Daddy," I said, trying to suppress my yawn so he'd stay longer. "I've been thinking."

"Yeah, Bean?" He sat on my bed, placed his hand on

my upper arm. His attention was all mine. No email or phone call was more important than this—our time together.

"Why can't you get another job? One that wouldn't take you away from us so much?"

"You know what I do is very important."

I didn't, in fact, know that. He consulted for big businesses or some such thing. "Yeah, but can't you do that here?"

He smoothed my hair with his thumb, his forehead crinkled. I noticed a few new wrinkles around his eyes. When did he get those? He wasn't that old. Quincy Matkin was my dad. He was going to live forever. "It's my job to provide a certain lifestyle for my family. For you and your mother."

"I wouldn't mind living in a shack as long as we were together. I'm sure Mom would be okay with that too."

"You're sure of that, are you?" He chuckled. "Aw, kid, I hope you never change."

"Why would I change, Daddy?"

He blinked, and it looked like he might actually cry —but I didn't think dads cried, so it made my stomach hurt a bit to see it. "Sometimes, the world changes you. Sometimes, other people's actions change you. Sometimes, you just make bad decisions. And then you find yourself between a rock and a hard place and don't know what to do, what decisions to make. The things you thought you wanted were ... well, not quite mistakes, but weren't the most honorable thing. And you don't know who you are anymore, but you do know one thing for certain."

I really didn't understand most of what he said, but the look of pure love, pure acceptance, in his eyes was something I knew I'd never be able to forget. "And what do you know for certain, Daddy?"

"That every second I spend apart from you, dear girl, tears me in half. I am never whole when I'm away from you."

"And Mom too, right?"

"Right." He grabbed me up into a hug, and I felt a plop of salty water fall onto my cheek. "I love you and your mother more than life, and as many things as I've done wrong, I hope you'll never forget that. I hope that this is the moment you hold onto, not all the mistakes I've made."

Oh, stars. I can't stop the sudden tears that are rolling down my cheeks as I sink against the wall.

"Alexis?" Someone says. It's a woman, but I'm blinded by my tears and don't know who. Kennedy? No, I'm not home. I'm on a cruise ship.

I push at the tears, and my hand comes away black with moistened mascara. Oh. It's Gloria, and she's gripping my upper arms, a look of concern on her face. "I'm f-fine. Sorry."

"Don't be sorry." She calls over her shoulder to Janet and Cecilia, something about finding someone. "Let's get you back to your room."

"No. I'm okay." I yank away. "You go back to your husband. Please, just …"

I can't be touched right now, not with the scalding

memory ramming around my heart and head, free at last after so many years.

"Alexis, I don't think you should be alone right now."

I swallow back the sobs threatening to burst from me again, force a smile. "I'm fine. See? But I do think I'll go lie down. Good night, Gloria."

And with her protests in my ears, I manage to make it to the elevators, down, down, down until I reach our floor, then take the hallway double-time before slapping my key card against our door lock, swinging open the door, and stepping inside.

Then I rip off my right shoe and chuck it as hard as I can at the window, screaming as the rage builds inside of me.

No! Dad doesn't get to say those things. Doesn't get to tell me—twenty-something years too late—that he's sorry. He never said it, but I can read beneath the surface of his words now that I know what I know.

Off comes the left shoe and *thunk*! It hits the window too and falls to the ground with an unsatisfying little plop.

And then the tears spill from my eyes again. Hard. I want to rip to shreds the memories that are coming— snippets of my dad and me, all the sweet times, the things he said that show me, yes, he did indeed love me, that he was sorry, but that he couldn't find a way to make what he'd done right, because it would have meant hurting or abandoning one of his daughters.

Maybe I can wash the memories away. Scrub them. Drown them.

I race to the shower, yank the curtain aside, twist it on full blast, and step into the icy stream fully clothed. Who cares if this dress is ruined? Who cares if my makeup bleeds down my face? Any of that is better than feeling this gut-wrenching pain of the truth I've always known but didn't want to accept crashing through my symptoms.

Someone bangs on the bathroom door. "Alexis? Are you okay?"

Dax.

Gloria or Janet or Cecilia must have told him I was upset. "Go away." My voice is ragged.

"Come out, Alexis. I'm a good listener, you know." A pause. "Just talk to me."

And suddenly, all my limbs are so tired. The water has turned warmer, almost scalding, and I yelp, shutting it down and then slumping to the ground against the bathroom counter. "I don't want to talk." I just want to sleep. He won't be able to handle my brand of crazy right now, that's for sure.

"Okay. We don't have to." His voice is low now, almost like he's sitting on the other side of this door. I can picture it, and the image is so sweet I nearly start crying again. "Please, Alexis. I just want to know that you're all right."

I'm not. That's what I want to say. I get the urge to tell him everything. But I'm not the light and fluffy version of Alexis, the sarcastic, the sexy. I'm the drenched-because-I-just-had-an-emotional-breakdown version. The I-just-took-a-shower-in-the-most-expensive-dress-I-own version. The I've-got-lots-of-baggage-and-you-should-run version.

And this version is A LOT to handle.

Frankly, I don't know if *I* want to handle this version of myself. I can't really expect my business partner in crime to do so.

Not even my friend.

But right now, he's all I have.

And, if I'm honest, he's all I want. And I'm too weak at the moment to resist that.

So I reach up and unlock the door. A few seconds after the click, he opens the door. His hair is mussed, like he's been running his hands through it. Jacket unbuttoned. His tie, askew.

"Well," I sniff. "Here I am. Your crazy pretend fiancée. What do you think?"

And Dax Nyhart squats down and places a hand on my arm. "I think some room service dessert is in order."

It's literally the perfect response—and that makes me start crying again.

In all honesty, I don't know if I ever felt this safe in Corbin's arms. But Dax? His arms are strong but loose enough that I don't feel trapped.

Dessert has been eaten, most of *Thor: Ragnarok* watched, our clothing changed to our pajamas. (After that first night of bare chested-ness, I made sure Dax wears a T-shirt with gym shorts to bed now because hi, don't need *that* temptation, thanks.) The credits roll across the dark screen, music lilting through the air until Dax switches the TV off, flooding our room with silence.

I don't remember how I found myself lying here with him, my back against his chest, tucked into his embrace while we watched the film, only that it happened in one fell swoop after the last bit of ice cream made it down my throat. Now that the movie is over, now that my adrenaline has run its course, I have no wish to move from here. To dissect all of this—both my freak out and what's happening between us. But I can't trust myself to know if this is real, or just the way Dax cares for his friends.

It makes me remember something he said the other day when discussing his mom. *"I just take care of my people, Alexis."*

Am I one of his people? Do I want to be? Even if he's leaving?

"Alexis." His voice goes soft as the hand that's touching me smooths my hair back, tucks it behind my ear. "You awake?" His head is propped on his elbow just behind my head, so I can tell he's looking down at me even if I can't see it.

In reply, I snuggle back against him, place my palms together and slip them under my cheek.

"If you want to talk about it, I'm here, you know."

"But not for long." The words are out before I can catch them. "I mean ..." I shut my eyes. Ugh. I don't want him thinking I'm pining over him, that I'm upset with him for his impending move. "This might surprise you, but I don't share my feelings very easily."

"I'm completely shocked," he deadpans. Then he chuckles, and the sound vibrates through my whole body.

"Ha ha." I wait, one, two, but the pressure is mounting in my chest, the need to speak—to share—fighting to get out. "I remembered something tonight. About … my dad."

He waits, seeming to understand I don't want a bunch of questions.

"See, um." I lick my lips in the semi-darkness. "The reason I'm so private, why I have a hard time letting people in …" A sob catches in my throat.

"It's okay, Alexis. You don't have to tell me."

My left hand leaves my right, trails down the mattress until it finds his resting against the sheets. "I want to. If that's all right."

He presses a light kiss against my hairline, and my toes flex at the contact which is all sweet friendship but sexy as anything. "Of course it's all right. I want to understand you. To know what makes you tick."

Oh. My. Stars. Is this man for real?

"I'm not sure we have that long," I joke, trying to break some of the tension.

"We"—he tightens his arms and laces our fingers together one by one—"have all the time in the world. Right now it's just us."

I remember what Kennedy said: *"At the very least, maybe he could be a friend."* And friends share their stuff, don't they? Even if one friend is moving away, you can still maintain a friendship long distance. What I tell him here, it won't be wasted.

"My dad died when I was thirteen. Plane crash. At his funeral, I found out …" I gulp down my fears. "I found out he had two families. Kennedy—my sister—she's his other daughter. By another woman."

"Dude." The word hangs in the air, suspended in disbelief. "I'm so sorry."

I squeeze his fingers and tug our hands up to my chin. With this movement, Dax stretches his legs downward and collapses his head onto the pillow, setting it against the back curve of my neck. His warm breath is making it hard to focus, but I do, because this is important.

I proceed to tell him all of it—the discovery, the funeral, meeting Kennedy, boarding school, moving to California, Corbin, about doing my best to survive with my heart intact. About failing, because once my trust is broken, it's hard for me to ever move past that.

And then I breathe, the weight lifted from my chest, emotions spilled across the space and time that exist only here in the bubble with Dax. "I just don't want to be anyone's fool ever again."

He's been quiet this whole time, letting me talk. And he's still not saying anything. "Did you fall asleep back there?" I release his hand, push away just slightly, and roll over to look at him.

Nope. Definitely not asleep. Even in the half-awake moonlight coming through the window, I see the serious way he's looking at me. The sobriety ringed with softness after all I've shared. "Alexis, you're the farthest thing from a fool. You're smart, cunning, and a vicious wordsmith when you're verbally sparring with someone."

I laugh softly.

"But you're also loyal. Your friends, your family, matter more to you than anything. And there's absolutely nothing foolish about loving with your whole heart."

"I haven't, though. That's just it. I've kept myself from so many people, because of what my dad did."

"And you're smart enough to realize now that that's not how you want to move forward. You're an evolving being, Alexis. You make mistakes. You learn. You grow. And you look fierce and beautiful doing it." He props his head up on his hand again, his bicep curving. "Not a fool."

I can't help but reach for him then, my fingers landing on his hip as I pull myself closer.

His breath catches.

So does mine.

For a long, terrible moment, neither of us speaks. We just blink at each other.

And wait. My lips tremble, aching with want to kiss this man. As for Dax? His face is a full-length novel condensed into ten seconds: surprise, joy, uncertainty, desire, abandonment, sadness.

Then, at last, he speaks. "You're an amazing woman, and some man is going to be freaking blessed to be with you." His lips lower and land on my … forehead. My stomach drops into a canyon.

Some man. But not him, right?

And whatever he says, I *have* been a freaking fool, thinking there was something between us. Am I so out of practice at this relationship thing that I don't even recognize when a guy is interested and when he isn't?

"Alexis ..."

Oh no. We're not having a let-her-down-easy talk. The only way to survive this is to go back to pretending. To hiding my emotions. What good did it do to let down my walls if the enemy decides the fortress isn't worth entering after all?

I give Dax a quick hug, then back away, sit up. "Thanks for listening tonight." I say it softly, so he knows at least that is true. My gratitude is real. He's been a friend, and that's all he ever promised to be. He hasn't done anything wrong here.

I'm the one who went and fell for her fake fiancé. Ugh. Looks like my heart didn't get the memo about the whole not-being-a-fool thing. But I will stay strong and stoic if it kills me.

I force a smile. "I'm going to hit the restroom and then I think a good, hard sleep is in order."

His jaw clenches, but he nods. "Yeah, whatever you need. I'm here."

I squeeze his arm. "I know."

fourteen

. . .

DESPITE THE ELECTRICITY of last night, the shock of Dax's rejection, I still woke up this morning fully rested, fully charged, for the first time in a long time.

Now it's Saturday around one o'clock. The cruise ends in two days. Dax said this morning he's going to wait until the last night to tell everyone the truth about us, so we don't ruin their vacation. He asked if I minded continuing the charade just a little longer. I mean, what else could I say but sure? If I told him the truth—*"No, I don't want to pretend to be in love with you when I might be falling in love for real because it's messing with my mind and I don't know what's true and what's for show"*—I'm not sure what he would say.

I don't want his pity or his rejection.

And then there's the part of me that really, really doesn't want it to end. That is okay with pretending, just a little longer. Because when we were in our room alone this morning, he didn't touch me. Not at all. But now that we are sitting on blankets on a beach in the Caribbean, the Bennetts and Meyers beside us, a floating water park in front of us?

Dax is holding my hand like it's his freaking job.

While I read from the tablet balanced in my lap—though, let's be honest, not much reading is actually going on—he's talking to Landon with my left hand in both of his. His thumbs absently stroke up and outward in opposite directions so the entire top of my hand is basically Dante's Inferno.

Squeals of delight have been echoing from the waterpark, which floats about fifty feet away from the beach. I squint and watch kids of all ages get their fill of the inflatable slides, the racing course, the trampoline. A dad helps a young girl climb the ladder from the water onto the yellow inflated surface. The ocean is calm and this exquisite blue color—I wonder if I could get my hair to match it? I'll have to check the store when I get home, see what color combos I can make.

Dax turns to me. "What are you thinking about?"

"I'm reading."

"You haven't flipped the screen in five minutes."

"Maybe I'm just a slow reader."

"Maybe"—his thumbs catch against my skin—"you want to go play on the waterpark with everyone else?"

I startle and glance up. Sure enough, Landon and Gloria are swimming out followed slowly by the Bennetts. "Should Gloria be doing that?"

"She said she's just going to get close and watch." He tugs my tablet away, sets it aside. "What do you say?"

I laugh. "Yeah, not really my thing. See how many people are out there?"

"Have you looked around us? This beach is getting more crowded by the minute."

My gaze roams the beach. Behind us, there's a hotel with a sand bar, music pumping, lots of chairs and umbrellas that were half empty when we got here a few hours ago. But he's right. Most of them are filled now and other than the towels our friends left behind, much of the beach space is swelling with the crowd. "Guess it shouldn't be surprising. It is the weekend."

"I've kind of forgotten what day is it, to be honest." He looks out at the ocean, and—maybe confirming that our friends are too far away to see us—drops my hand, then swivels his body so we are facing each other cross-legged, our knees touching. "It'll be a trip to go back to work after this, huh?"

"Yeah." I find a small stick in the sand and poke at the tiny granules. A hole forms but fills in quickly as the surrounding grains fall back into place. "I can't believe it's already almost the holidays. What are your plans for Thanksgiving?"

"Mom and I will go to my aunt and uncle's. I'll see my cousins. The usual. What about you?"

"My friends and I usually do Friends-giving sometime around the actual holiday. This year, we're doing it Friday at my place. Kennedy was supposed to come up this week, but she's already there." I drop the stick. "In fact, I need to check in with her before I get back on the boat."

"Yeah, I need to check in with Mom too." He cocks

his head. "Speaking of moms ... you don't mention yours much. Do you guys talk?"

I shrug. "Like, the basics. Birthdays, holidays. But she married my dad's old business partner when I was in high school and has resumed her position in the Connecticut socialite circles."

"Guessing you guys don't have a lot in common then."

Placing my hand against my chest, I say in my best snooty voice, "What ever could you mean, darling? You don't find me completely droll and sophisticated?"

"I find you completely something, all right." His eyes are liquid brown, burning.

My hand stills, contracts, then travels back to my lap. "Yeah, well, you're right. We're nothing alike."

"You mentioned boarding school. Seemed you didn't like it there very much." He moves a finger through the sand. "Are you mad at her for sending you?"

"Like, do I hold a grudge?"

He nods.

"Not really. She's never been the kind of woman who could survive without a man. So when my dad died—and she found out about Pippa and Kennedy—she couldn't function. Made me decide right then and there that I would never depend on a man for my happiness, though."

Dax stiffens momentarily at the remark, but keeps an impassive face. "You're such a strong woman. I can't see you ever falling apart."

"Uh, are you completely blocking last night's incident from your brain?" Because I definitely can't.

A smile quirks the corner of his lips. "No. But look at you today. You're fine again. We're all going to have weak moments, Alexis. And personally, I think it's good to have people in our corner to help pick us up. Not that we can't do it by ourselves, but why would you want to go through life without support when it can make such a difference?"

His words find their target, smashing into some of the final bricks holding the fortress around my heart in place. "Look who's talking, Dax."

"What's that supposed to mean?"

I soften my tone. "Just that you could also use the reminder that you don't have to do everything yourself. If your uncle is helping out with your mom, if he helped out in the past, then that means he wants to."

"It's not his job, though."

"It's not completely yours, either. Your mother is a grown woman. And your dad was wrong to put that on you."

Dax shifts, but doesn't say anything.

"I mean it. You've been killing yourself trying to prove something, maybe that you're better than your dad was. I don't know. All I know is that when he left you that note saying you needed to be the man of the house, he told you what kind of man to be. You grew up in his crooked shadow." I poke his knee lightly with my stick. "But guess who gets to decide what kind of man you are? You. And from what I can see, you're doing a wonderful job. So just … I don't know. Accept the support if it's being offered, I guess. You're lucky you have it."

When I get the courage to glance up at him, his jaw is slack and he's staring at me. Still not speaking.

I reach for my phone. "Speaking of support, I need to be Kennedy's."

Dax clears his throat. "How about a game before you call her?"

Clearly he wants to change the subject just as badly as I do. Checking the clock on my phone, I shrug and slip it back into my bag. "I guess I've got time. What did you have in mind?"

He leans back on his hands. "We haven't played Truth or Dare yet."

"No way. I hated that game growing up."

"Why?"

I roll my eyes. "Because when girls play it, the Truth questions are always about which boy you like, who you've made out with, your deepest darkest secrets, and whether you pee in the shower."

His eyebrows shoot up as he laughs. "And the Dares?"

"Stupid things like eating some gross concoction, putting on makeup without looking and walking around the mall like that, running through someone's back yard without any clothes on."

"Yeah, sounds about right in my experience too, except for the makeup part." He grins, and a little bit of me melts. It's the sun. It's hot out and—yeah, fine. Dax is quickly becoming my sun, and I both hate and love it. When he sits forward, I can't help but move a tiny fraction of an inch that way too. "Okay, what if I promise not to dare you to do any of that? Then will you play?"

"You're assuming I'd pick Dare."

"All right." Something flashes in his eyes. "I also promise not to ask you which boy you like." He leans even closer, his elbows on his knees. "Or whether you pee in the shower."

I make a face. "Gross."

"Especially because we're sharing a shower right now."

My face hurts from smiling. "Fine, I'll play your dumb little game. Only to pass the time until everyone gets back, though."

He rubs his hands together, delighted like a kid who just got a bunch of toys and doesn't know which one to play with first. "Truth or Dare?"

"Truth. Duh."

Stroking his chin, he studies a palm tree nearby. "Got it. If you had the superpower of invisibility, what's the worst thing you'd do?"

"Ooo, you're devious. I like it."

Dax puffs out his chest. "Why thank you."

"Hmm." When a picture pops into my head, I giggle —hard. "I'd waltz into Adolf's office and cut off the ends of that horrible mustache."

Dax crumples forward with laughter, and I join him. Oh man, this feels good, to let loose with someone who gets it. Who gets me.

All because I've let him see me this week, really see who I am under all the layers.

"Your turn. Truth or Dare?"

"I'll do Truth as well."

"Really." I tap my lips. "Surprising."

"I'm full of surprises, Alexis." He says my name like warm chocolate and it's all I can do not to literally fan myself.

I resume possession of the stick at my side, rolling and pinching it between my fingers as I think. "What's one thing you'd never do for all the money in the world?"

"Cheat on a woman."

My head rears back at how quickly his answer came, at the steadiness of his gaze. It undoes me from the inside out. "G-good answer."

"It's the truth."

Looking away, I shove the stick into the ground so hard it scratches my palm. No blood, thankfully, and the pain is good—a reminder that no matter what I think Dax is saying with his eyes, he made it very clear last night that he is not the man for me. "I'll take Dare this time."

"Surprising me right and left, I see."

"I'm full of surprises, Dax." I parrot his words back to him, both a tease and a challenge in them.

"Oh, I don't doubt it." He stands and holds out his hands to me. "Your dare is to join me out at the waterpark."

"You were building to this the whole time, weren't you?" I let him haul me to my feet, dusting off the shorts covering my bikini bottoms.

"Of course not."

"Uh huh. I don't believe you."

Laughing, he starts tugging me toward the water.

"Wait." I tug my shorts off and leave them on the blanket. "Sorry. I didn't want them to get wet."

A thrill shoots through me at the way his jaw ticks. "Right." Then he tugs his shirt over his head. "Good idea."

Have mercy. "Um, well … let's go then."

We wade into the water and swim toward the waterpark. Halfway there, we encounter the Bennetts and Meyers, who apparently have had enough fun.

"Oh, sorry, loves!" Janet squawks, floating with ease thanks to the life vest squeezed over her large bosom. "It's not exactly made with old people in mind."

Cecilia's arms glide through the water as she doggy paddles in place. "My knees started aching after one minute. But you two have fun. We'll let you know when it's time to head back to the boat."

"Oh, we can head back with you now," I say.

Dax clucks his tongue. "A dare's a dare, RB."

Fred roars with laughter. "You'd best be listening to your man, Ms. Matkin. Go on, you youngsters. We'll watch from where we can't injure ourselves anymore."

"Speak for yourself," Tom adds. "I have delicate skin and the sun hates me."

We all have a good chuckle while they head back and we move closer to the waterpark. There are several rope ladders ringing the outside and inside of the huge inflatable, which is arranged in a few intersecting circles. A dark-skinned lifeguard sits on a Wave Runner between the beach and the waterpark in case anyone needs help, but we all had to sign waivers stating we understood not every inch of this waterpark would be visible to the lifeguard at once and that, while kids were required to wear the provided life vests, adults didn't have to. Not sure that would stand in the States, but every country has its rules, I guess, and a waiver is a waiver.

Personally, I'm kind of glad to not be restrained by one, plus I feel one hundred percent confident in my swimming ability. In Dax, whose strokes are strong.

We reach the platform quickly, and it's definitely not as crowded as it's been, likely because the excursion is almost over, so when I hoist myself onto the surface, there's a sense of freedom I didn't expect. It feels both as if we are far away from the world and a part of it.

Then the rest of the world fades and it's just Dax and me jumping on the trampoline like we're twelve. Then we're running along the hard but bouncy surface, which is only about three feet wide. Dax chases me as I squeal and try to balance, arms out, before falling back into the water.

He dives in after me. "You okay?"

I laugh and splash him in the face. "I can swim, silly. And it's not *that* deep."

He slicks back his hair and we climb up again, cannonballing into the ocean over and over. After several minutes, we make our way to the racing course. "You ready to eat my dust, RB?" Leaning forward, I get a nice visual of his muscles all taut and ready for action.

"Oh, Booger Bear, you're so adorable when you're wrong." I grin. "Go!"

I only see him out of the corner of my eye, but my braid hops and falls against my back as I run, and it seems we're neck in neck when we climb an inflatable angled wall, slide down the opposite side, leap from circle to circle, swing over open water to the finish line —where we land at the exact same time at the back edge of the park.

Doesn't stop me from pretending I won though. Lifting my hands Rocky style, I do a little shuffle. "How did it feel to lose, Nyhart?"

"Wouldn't know, Matkin." His eyes flash dangerously at me as he slinks closer. "I'm sure you had a pleasant enough experience watching my backside the whole time, though."

I yelp in protest and push him overboard like he deserves. But he must anticipate my move, because his hand sneaks around me and pulls me with him.

The shock of the water has me gasping when I bob right back up, and I kick toward the ladder latched to the opposite end of the inflatable, which is still on the back of the waterpark, facing away from the beach. Once I'm there, I hold on with one hand to the ladder while I wait for Dax to catch up.

When he does, he's sputtering with laughter. "I feel like we've been in the water more than we've been up there." He's treading water in front of me and I can't help but be mesmerized by his powerful shoulders as they move.

But I snap out of it quickly, put on a sardonic pout. "You need a rest, old man?"

He swims up, grabs the ladder too, his handhold just below mine. "Maybe I do." And suddenly we're close, inches apart, really, and he's drawing slowly, softly nearer, the movement splashing a tiny wave of water up my chest. I don't even realize I'm moving until my back is flush with the ladder, and Dax is directly in front of me, gripping the ropey side rails on either side of my head.

When he pulls himself forward, my knees brush his rib cage and my arms do the thinking for me, letting go of the rope and finding themselves around his neck so we are a pretzel, woven together, waiting to be broken—because maybe this is all for show. Not that the Bennetts can exactly see us, but considering he didn't touch me this morning, didn't kiss me last night, what else can I assume?

In this moment, though, I can't be bothered to care about that. I only care about here. Now.

Dax.

He gently pushes my body against the ladder, getting as close as he can, and hooks his feet into the bottom rung of the ladder that's below the surface. I definitely know he's got me when one arm slips under the ladder and yet also around my waist. There isn't much bobbing or splashing of the water here in this bay. It's calm, unlike the rapid beating of my heart as Dax's face hovers an inch from mine.

"Hi," he says.

"Hi."

Our shallow breaths linger in the space between us, which grows smaller by the second. When his nose touches mine, his wet hair dripping droplets onto my cheeks, I can feel the phantom kiss hanging there, can practically taste it. His head bobs away slightly and I chase it, then retreat. We are all inhalations and limbs tangled but the tension is pooling inside of me and I might crack with it if this man doesn't kiss me soon.

And then, finally, the stars collide and his lips touch mine. Tentative. Soft. Sweet.

I sigh into him, and that's all it takes for his mouth to move more urgently, to press a little deeper, to open in invitation. My hands bulldoze up into his hair, fingers streaking and tugging as they run a course they've been dying to try for weeks—maybe months, if I'm completely honest with myself.

His hands may be engaged with keeping us afloat, but his lips more than make up for it as they wander across my jaw, feathering their way to my ear, my neck. I arch into him, groaning a bit when he reaches the hollow above my collarbone. "Dax."

He pulls back, looks at me. "What are you doing to me, Alexis?"

With a fingertip, I trace his eyebrows, his nose, his lips, the outer shell of his ear. "I'm finally playing the game."

His hand flexes where it's securing my hip to the ladder. "RB ..."

"It's okay." I lean forward, kissing a ring around his ear, and his body shudders against me. "Just kiss me, Dax. Please."

"So polite." A smile spreads across his face.

"I can be more forceful if you'd like." I lock my hands around his neck again and draw his head close, so our lips are hovering once again. "Kiss me, Dax. *Now.*"

"Yes, ma'am."

And he does, so hard and fast that if I wasn't closing my eyes, I'd be seeing stars. Every bit of space between us is eaten up, gone, and I just want it to be him and me forever. As his lips crash into mine, I'm hot and aflame, scorching and freezing all at once. I gasp at his fervency, at the little growl he makes, at the way his hands—

"There you guys are—whoa."

Dax vaults back from the ladder at the sound of Landon's voice above us. I peek up, my chest heaving with exertion. With the thought that I might be in love.

Oh my goodness.

I let go of the ladder, dunk myself under the water to attempt to cool off. When I come back up, Dax is waiting. Landon's gone. He holds out his hand. "Everyone's ready to get back on the ship. Are we ... good?"

It's hard to tell where his head is at. Is he as dazed as I am? Does he want this too? Want me? It certainly seemed like it. But he's not saying anything, not clarifying.

Maybe he will. Once he's had time to process. I need that time too. Must call my people.

So I shuck on a smile and grab his hand. "Yeah. We're good."

Man, I hope so, anyway.

fifteen

. . .

I'VE FELT underwater all night, all day, trying to catch my breath, trying to see despite the proverbial salt stinging my eyes and clouding my vision. The last thirty hours have been a mix of ecstasy and anguish, their uncertainty a fine form of torture like a needle piercing flesh—so small it's hard to pinpoint, like acupuncture that is a painful benediction. And you're never quite sure if it's healing or harming.

But I've survived.

After the kiss yesterday afternoon, Dax and I parted ways and I called Kennedy. Couldn't reach her, so I wandered the market until it was nearly time to board the ship. Tried again. Finally got her, only to find her in tears because she and Brooks broke up for good.

I'm not exactly sad—I was never his biggest fan, but I *am* hers, and so I'm sorry she's suffering. Promised to be there as quickly as I can on Monday, then put in a quick call to Shelby asking for her to take care of

Kennedy. She's on Thanksgiving break at work all week and assured me she would stand in the gap until I got home.

So yeah. Didn't exactly get the pep talk I was looking forward to and needed from my little sister. In fact, I got a grisly reminder of the inconstancy of men.

Some men, anyway. Dax has never given me reason to believe he would be like Brooks or any other jerk I've had in my own life. But he hasn't told me how he's feeling either—whether that kiss meant anything to him like it did to me.

Oh sure, he's spent the entire day with me, by my side as we read near the pool, ate burgers and fries, watched Landon and Gloria continue to schmooze with the Bennetts. But last night after dinner he stayed out late and I went to bed early. This morning, he was gone to the gym again before I got up.

And even when we got ready for dinner this afternoon, he gave me my space, showering quickly and then saying he was meeting Tom and Fred for some drinks. I wondered if he was going to tell them we aren't really engaged—it's the last night on the ship, after all—but no one treated me any differently over dinner. The women laughed and cooed and hugged me and it made me sad to know it would all be ending soon.

Very soon.

Maybe Dax is determined to not find time for the conversation at all. Everyone else has gone off to bed, but here we are on the upper deck, watching a movie under the stars. We're sharing a long beach chair that's sitting upright, with Dax behind me, his arms around my waist, legs on either side of me, nose nuzzling the back of my ear as my head leans back against him. Of course, we had settled in this position when the movie started, but one by one our party left for bed.

Now it's just us and a few other random couples peppered throughout the deck, bags of popcorn sitting forgotten on our side table as the movie credit music sweeps over us. The sky is a deep midnight, edged and dotted with silver, and I'm not sure how it's possible, but I can smell land approaching.

The end is nigh.

I wonder if Dax dreams about staying here forever just like I do, in a bubble where he and I make sense, where the fear of the past repeating itself doesn't interfere with the future, where we don't have to deal with the fact he's moving away and this might all be dead before it's even begun.

Or maybe it really is all in my head. Maybe that kiss really was just for show.

On the screen, a new movie begins—didn't know this was a double feature—and my body relaxes even more against him. We've been gifted another few hours. I don't even care that what we're watching appears to be a rom-com, a thought that makes me giggle.

"What?" Dax murmurs against my skin.

I shiver at his nearness. "Just looks like your kind of movie."

"I can go ask them to change it to something about an ax murderer if you prefer."

"That would be lovely. Thanks."

His chuckle presses his lips against my neck and we watch like that, my body a live wire that's aware of every place it touches his. The brief opening credits are cute, with curly fonts and bright colors, and the story begins, predictably, with the lead character walking in on her cheating ex.

I groan. "Make it stop."

Dax squeezes me against him. "Is this too painful to watch?"

"Yes! Ugh, kill me now."

He doesn't laugh, is waiting, and I realize he's really asking if I'm okay. "Oh! Because of Corbin?"

His nod is a brush of nose against neck.

"No." I turn to face him, one leg up on the seat, the other touching the ground. And as remiss as I am to leave our cozy nest, I want to talk more. "Can we go where it isn't so loud?"

"Okay."

We get up, head through the lido deck to the other side of the ship, by the pool where the group found me reading what feels like months ago. It's deserted—eerily so—and the ocean sparkles under the moonlight as the ship cuts through it. We watch the wake from the thick white railing until I'm ready to broach the subject of Corbin again.

"So unlike that movie, I did not catch my ex in the act of cheating or anything, though I did see them together a year ago at a restaurant. They were married and she was already pregnant." I massage my temple against the memory. "I found out about his affair when I thought we were going to pick out engagement rings, and he broke up with me in the jewelry store parking lot."

"I hate him for you."

My lips quirk. "Whoa there, tiger. Slow your roll." I lean sideways against the railing, facing him. "I asked him if there was someone else and he said yes. So unfeeling, until he made his impassioned cries about how I didn't give him enough of what he wanted." At Dax's arched eyebrow, I shake my head. "Not *that*. He was talking about my heart."

"Hmm. Still hate him." He faces me too. "Don't you?"

"No."

"Do you still love him then?"

What a question. Thankfully, I can answer him honestly, even if I can't look him in the eye while doing it. My eyes drift to his chest, solid beneath his tight shirt. "I related a lot to what you said about Lilith, about playing the wrong game. The thing is, Corbin was safe. I didn't realize it at the time, but he was the slot machines —low buy-in, not a lot of risk, not a lot of reward. That probably sounds terrible." I bite my lip. "He blamed me, you know. For his cheating."

"I've got a word for him," Dax huffs out. It's cute the way he's defending me.

I smile briefly, but it stretches and cracks against my lips. "He said I never loved him the way he loved me. That he deserved someone who needed him, who wanted him in the same way. Who kissed him like she meant it." I tug my braid forward, study it. The blue has faded over the week, and I think it's the longest I've kept my hair a single color in … well, a long time. "Maybe he's right. Maybe I should have done better."

"And what do *you* deserve? For some guy to treat you like garbage?" His fingers tilt my chin up to meet his gaze again. "No. *You're* the right kind of game, Alexis. You're high-stakes poker—hard to win, but with a potentially life-changing reward."

Okay, I'm definitely not imagining this thing between us. It is real and full and maybe about to become the thing we finally talk about.

I swallow hard. Step toward him like Peggy Carter drawn to Steve Rogers across time and space. "Dax, that has to be the sweetest …" Tears prick my eyes.

"I know we both started all of this saying we weren't looking for anything, another relationship. But Alexis, I've fallen for you. Hard." His hands gently cup my face, a thumb sweeping away a tear as it falls. "You've always intrigued me, but getting to know you this week —now it's so much more. You challenge me to think about the world differently. You make me the most real version of myself and even though it's hard to be vulnerable, I want to be that. For you."

My breath is gone. Just … gone.

"And I know the men in your life have disappointed you. But do you think you could be ready to try again … with me?"

Oh, Dax. How did he turn from my enemy into the person I want to be around most? The first guy I could see myself throwing away all my inhibitions for? Really and truly loving? And yet … "Even if I was, you're leaving. Moving to Texas. How would that even work?"

"There are these fancy new devices called cell phones and airplanes—"

"Stop." I push against his chest, but his hands hook my waist and draw me back against him. "Long distance is no joke."

"It wouldn't be easy. I know that." His brow furrows. "I think this could be worth the effort, though."

"If you felt this way, then why …" I whisper as his face draws toward mine. "Why didn't you kiss me the other night?"

"You mean after you finally opened up and told me about your dad, your ex?"

I nod.

"I wanted to. You don't even know." He rests his forehead against mine and strings a piece of loose hair behind my ear. "But you were in a vulnerable place and I didn't want to take advantage. Didn't want to scare you off."

The vise gripping my ribcage releases. It makes so much sense now. He wasn't rejecting me. He was protecting me. "You wouldn't have."

"So"—he breathes—"can we make a go of this? I plan to break the news about us to the Bennetts over breakfast tomorrow, but we still have one more night before we have to face reality. Before we have to figure all of this out."

"Do you have to tell them, now that we're kind of together?" I lift hopeful eyebrows. That would solve so many problems. LA is still not San Diego, but it's so much closer than Texas.

"RB." He says it softly, a bit chastising, before kissing first one eyebrow, then the other.

"You're right. I know." We should never have lied in the first place. But then we wouldn't be here, in this place either. Even blessings can come from mistakes.

Just like Kennedy. She was my dad's mistake—but she's been my biggest blessing.

I run my hand down the length of his shirt collar, stop at the top button. Arch up on my tiptoes and press a kiss into the hollow of his neck, where his five o'clock scruff is rough against my lips. Something rumbles in his chest and his mouth meets mine, a gentle pressure filled with all the sweet things.

Promises.

Hope.

Maybe even love.

Dax pulls back, smiles, and looks like he's about to kiss me again when someone calls his name. We turn and look at Tom, who is wheezing a bit and waving his arm. His face is red and he bends over, hands on his knees.

When we reach him, I place a hand on his shoulders. "What's wrong?"

"Couldn't … find … you. Split … up." His wheezes start to slow as I rub circles on his upper back. Then he stands, looks into Dax's concerned face. "The cruise line has … been trying to reach you for a while. Called our room."

His expression goes slack. "Why?"

Tom pulls a kerchief from his back pocket, mops his

wide brow. "Some woman named Lilith has been calling nonstop trying to get ahold of you."

The information smacks me between the eyes. I blink. "Lilith."

"Yes. I remember because I thought it such a pretty name, like a delicate flower."

"Ha." She's delicate all right, in the way a weed is delicate. Blows in the wind, could snap in half, but apparently, she keeps coming back. I cross my arms over my chest and look at Dax. "You're still talking to her?"

"What? No." He runs a hand through his hair.

"Then why in the world would she be calling you on a cruise ship of all things? How does she even know you're here?"

"I have no idea. Seriously, Alexis, you have to believe me."

Tom shifts from one foot to the other, clearly just now realizing that Lilith might be a sore subject. "I think I'll just—"

"Don't leave, Tom." Oops, didn't exactly mean to yell at him, but I cannot be alone with Dax right now or I might do something drastic like push him overboard. My fists clench at my sides as I step toward Dax, finger pointed at his chest. "As for you, no, I don't have to believe you. Obviously, you haven't earned my trust like I thought."

"Can we just go see what she wants?"

"Sure, yeah. Just go ahead with Tom. I'm going to our room."

His jaw loosens. "I'll come right there and tell you what's going on." He starts to follow Tom.

"Don't bother," I mutter.

Turning, Dax stalks back toward me. "I'm not your dad. I'm not Corbin."

But maybe he is, my subconscious whispers.

Fool me once, fool me twice … But fool me three times?

"The fact that Lilith knew how to reach you says otherwise." I shut my eyes to his pleading gaze, then reopen, my stoic stare engaged. "It's not like you did anything wrong, Dax. We were together for all of one minute. Shortest relationship I've ever been in, but then again, it sounds like you just saved me a lot of time and energy." Pulling away, I pivot to leave.

"So you're just going to leave?" He voice cracks a bit. Maybe he's thinking of his dad, who slipped away without a word. Or Lilith, who left him. But no. I can't go feeling sorry for him, not if he's still in contact with his ex-fiancée. Not if he's lying to me about *that*. And even if he isn't, what if she wants him back? What if he didn't mean all the stuff he said about not really being in love with Lilith?

What if, with me, he got swept away in the pretense too? Maybe it would have happened with whoever he decided to take on this trip as his fake fiancée. Maybe it has nothing to do with who I am and everything to do with our circumstances. Maybe I was only ever a rebound for the real woman he wanted.

But I won't be like my dad. I won't give in to a mistake that creates more problems for me in the future, not when there are warning signs all over the place.

"I know you, Alexis. You fight for what you want."

Dax takes a step toward me. "So is it really so easy for you to walk away like this?"

Easy? Is he serious? I look up at him, my heart pinching, my subconscious asking if maybe I'm wrong. (Make up your freaking mind there, dude!) But here's the crux of it. I could have loved him, yes. Which means he, more than anyone, has the potential to storm my heart, to chisel it down piece by piece over the years until there's nothing left.

Though honestly, in this moment, the chisel has sliced right through my connective tissue. He's hit the hammer only once and the pieces of my heart litter the entire back deck of this ship. The whole ocean is filled with the broken remnants of my regret.

"You just made it easy for me," I lie. Shaking my head, I turn to a very bewildered Tom. I set my hand on his arm, force a smile. "Thank you for everything. And … I'm sorry."

Then I start walking, hear Tom: "What's going on, son?"

Dax sighs. Hesitates a long moment. "I was going to tell you this tomorrow morning, but Alexis isn't—"

His words cut away as I blow through the doors toward the elevators.

Toward escape.

Toward safety.

Toward a life of me, myself, and I.

And maybe a cat.

sixteen

· · ·

"POOR SIS," Kennedy says as she slips her arm around my shoulders the next day. "It's been a long few weeks, huh?"

Long doesn't begin to cover it. My Uber just dropped me off from the airport five minutes ago. After allowing me to use the restroom and set my suitcase in my room, Kennedy pulled me back into the living room to talk. But I don't want to talk. I'm exhausted from a sleepless night alone—when I got back to the room, I slipped Dax's suitcase into the hallway and slapped the dead-bolt in place—and a full day of solo travel. I woke up too late to say goodbye to the Bennetts, and I didn't see Dax on my flight. Must mean he caught an earlier or later one.

Which, really, is for the best. It's bad enough I'll have to see him tomorrow and Wednesday at work. So maybe I'll just take the whole rest of the week off. Not sure how my client load is going, though …

Argh. My brain is mush. "Ken, I really don't w—"

"Wait, don't tell me anything yet. I'm woman enough to admit that I will not give you great advice at the moment thanks to the Stooks situation." That's what we're calling her ex. Stands for Stupid Brooks. "We need reinforcements." Kennedy leaps from the couch and calls down the hallway. "Shelby, Lauren!"

A few minutes later, my two housemates saunter into the living room, pulling up short when they see me.

They react simultaneously. "Alexis, you're home!" "Lexi Lou … what's wrong?" Then my housemates fling themselves onto the couch on either side of me and grab my hands. Shelby nestles down onto my shoulder, giving me a half hug.

Immediately, the air feels a little easier to breathe.

"Girls," Kennedy says, "I've called Evie and Kayla for backup"—the doorbell rings—"and that would be them now."

How did my sister know I'd need them? I haven't told her anything yet, haven't even talked with her except to message her that I was getting on my flight. As if she can hear my thoughts, she turns when she reaches the door. "Your text sounded sad."

My text said, *On the way home. Be there by four.* It was devoid of the emojis she's so fond of.

But sad. Sure.

My sister just might be the most perceptive person I know after all. Either that or it's simply a result of belonging to the generation that thinks if you use proper grammar in your texts, you're either mad or sad.

Kennedy opens the door and in waddle my two

pregnant buddies. Kayla has a bottle of wine in one hand, margarita mix in the other, both of which she deposits on the coffee table. "Just in case."

I snort. "Uh, Kay. Need I remind you that you can't have any of that?"

"You think I need a reminder?" She raises an eyebrow. "This is how you know I love you."

A small smile inches onto my lips.

Evie contributes a bag of Reese's Pieces so large it could feed a whole circus crew. "Don't tell Connor I stole his emergency supply. But desperate times, right?"

"Ooo, brave woman," Lauren crows. She vacates the couch so Evie can sit comfortably, taking the floor instead.

Meanwhile, Kayla lowers herself into the overstuffed chair, her descent so slow it looks like she's doing an intense squat. When she catches me staring, she glares. "You try making this look graceful—and not peeing yourself in the process—when you've got a watermelon growing inside of you."

I hold up my hands. "I didn't say a thing."

She mumbles something under her breath, adjusts herself, then studies me. "So. Did you take my advice?"

Figures she would start there. I just lay my head back against the couch, close my eyes.

"You did!"

Then the chatter erupts all around me. "You kissed him?" "Are you together?" "Was this a fake kiss or a not fake kiss? Because I've had both of those and sometimes there's not really a difference!" "Did he get the job?"

"You guys, stop." That would be Shelby. She squeezes my hand. "Alexis, why are you crying?"

Am I? With a check of my cheeks, sure enough my fingers come away wet. I open my eyes and bite my lip —which is swollen from all the gnawing I've done lately—at the wide eyes, the compassion, the love staring back at me. "Um." I swallow. "A lot has happened."

"We're here if you want to talk." Evie reaches for a tissue on the side table and nearly rolls over sideways with the effort. Once she's snagged one, she places it in my hand. "Or we can find some savage, homicidal movie to watch together if that would make you feel better."

I laugh through my tears. "It would. It really would."

Next to me, Shelby looks rather terrified but nods. "Of course that's what we should do. Lauren? Ice cream!"

"On it!" Lauren starts to stand, but I hold up my hand.

"No, wait."

My friends freeze. I pull a strip off the tissue, little white flecks falling away onto my jeans. "I'd like to tell you guys what happened." All day, my brain has been warring with my heart, wondering if I was right to leave. Maybe my friends, who each had to go through stuff to find their way to love, will be able to see things more clearly than I can.

"We're all ears, Sis." Kennedy sits back against the entertainment center, her eyes never leaving me. It doesn't matter that she's going through heartache right now. She sees me. She's got me, just like I've got her.

By the time I've told them everything, the tissue Evie gave me is in shreds on my lap.

Kayla's face is screwed up with concentration as she taps her manicured nails against the arm of the chair. "So did you ever find out why Lilith called Dax?"

"No. But doesn't it seem suspicious that she knew he was there?"

"So many things might seem suspicious to someone who is already predisposed to find fault with a situation," Kennedy offers. "Like you with relationships."

"What does she mean?" Lauren asks. "Why are you predisposed?"

Oh, ugh. I don't know if I have the energy to go through all of that. But Kennedy's eyes are soft on me. She doesn't ask in words, but she doesn't have to. I nod, and she gently explains about Corbin. About our dad.

The room is silent for a bit. "I don't want your sympathy, guys."

"Well"—Kayla pipes up—"you can have my empathy. Looks like we've both got daddy issues, girl."

"You're one step ahead of me." Lauren shrugs. "I don't even have a dad."

"And obviously I don't really remember much about ours." That would be Kennedy.

I look around this room—at each of my friends. Even the ones who have loving fathers have lost someone important to them. They've all had to struggle, to grow, to forgive themselves, forgive others.

Warmth floods my heart and I take the biggest strip

of tissue—and it's not big—and try to wipe under my eyes, which are drizzling again. Because I was wrong. I've not lost them. These friends dropped what they had going on today to be here with me. And no matter how much things have changed, we are family. The kind that sticks together no matter how many husbands and babies and jobs and moves come into the picture. I sniffle. "I don't know how I got so lucky to be part of this group."

"Well, you had the house. With your lime-green hair and crazy eyes, we wouldn't have come near you with a ten-foot pole otherwise."

"Kayla!" Evie laughs, hands me another tissue. "What our very loving but often emotionally obtuse friend here is trying to say is, we love you too."

"Someone pull out your phone and Google 'obtuse,'" Kayla declares.

I don't exactly know why it's so funny, but we're all laughing. After my sides protest, I stop. We settle. Then Kennedy breaks the quiet again as she pulls her knees into her chest. "I know Dad hurt you, Sis. But it really seems like you've been finally dealing with it, wrestling with that pain, not letting it get you down anymore. Not in the same way, at least."

"Yeah, I have." The tissue is soft against my cheeks as I wipe away the salty residue drying there. I turn to the rest of my friends, to explain. "All this time, I assumed that because my dad lied to us about why he was always leaving, he was also lying about loving me. But I've been trying to understand what really happened. And while I don't know that I could go as far as to say I'm glad for it, or even that I fully forgive what he did, I do think that I can accept it now. Accept that, in his own ways, he cared for me."

"I'm proud of you," Kayla says. Her dad left when she was young, so she more than anyone really can empathize. "It's not a one-and-done thing, but if you're willing to let go of the bitterness, forgiveness will come." All joking aside, she smiles softly.

Thank you, I mouth.

Anytime, she mouths back.

"We're all proud of you." Shelby pats my knee.

"We are." Evie pumps my hand tight again in solidarity. "But can I suggest something? I think for your own peace of mind, you need to find out what happened with Dax. Maybe you're right and he really was seeing Lilith on the side, or lying to you about what was happening." She purses her lips, her eyes going some other place, like she's remembering. "But sometimes there are things beneath the surface that you won't know unless you follow your man to a garden and find out exactly what went wrong." Her vision clears and she seems to notice that she went off script a bit. "For example."

"And what if I was wrong?" The thought shoots fiery fear into my veins. "He will never want to see me again."

"I know you think you're above such things, Sis, but we all make mistakes," Kennedy teases. "If you were wrong, you find a way to apologize. To make it right."

"I'm not used to that." And it's not because I'm perfect by any means, not because I don't make mistakes. But other than Kennedy and the occasional tiff with one of my friends here, I haven't really cared enough about anyone *to* apologize.

But Dax …

I don't know how to find out the truth other than to ask him, but that seems like circular thinking. But a few hours later, after a dinner of Ben & Jerry's with my besties, I get an idea. It might not pan out. They might not have the information I need.

But either way, I need to make several apologies. And this is where I will start.

seventeen

. . .

I CAN COUNT on one hand the number of times I've been this nervous.

First day of boarding school. First day working at Birmingham. First day each of my roommates moved in.

And now, seeing Dax again.

The elevator pings open on my floor and I step out, adjusting my beanie before heading toward the Birmingham suite. From the sterile hallway, I catch a glimpse of Gina talking with one of the Drs. Strange at her desk. I press into the door and it swings open, along with Gina's eyes.

"Alexis. You're back." Her lips drop into a flat line as she reaches for a Hershey's kiss. "You look rather tan." Not sure how she can know that, considering I'm wearing a long-sleeved blouse and pants, but whatever. I suppose my collarbone and neck *are* showing. She continues. "I didn't think it was *that* sunny in San Francisco." Guess some things haven't changed since I left.

My coworkers don't know I went on a cruise with Dax. We didn't want to start needless rumors—though if it's up to me, rumors *will* be started this day. I just don't know how he feels about that, which is why my fingers are so tingly I'm afraid they might fall off.

I slip on a grin. "Lovely as always to see you, Gina dear." Kill 'em with kindness, right? Taking a piece of her chocolate, I continue down the hall, ignoring her comment to what's-his-name about how suspicious I look with my hair all tucked under my hat like that and did he *see* the smirk I was wearing?

When I get to my office, I unlock it and step inside, greeted by the musty smell of disuse. "Ah, home sweet home," I mutter.

I purposefully got in earlier than usual today so I could be ready. Start up my computer. Go get some water from the front dispenser. Begin checking my emails.

But I can't focus.

My eyes blur as I stare at the screen. Flit to the clock. It's only been ten minutes.

I groan and peek down the hallway. No Dax in sight. Isn't he usually here by now? Oh no. What if he doesn't come in today? Or tomorrow? What if he's already resigned or moved to Texas or—

Nate. Of course.

For once, Nate being Dax's uncle is a blessing. I stand so quickly that my knee hits the top of my desk. After hopping around in pain for a few seconds, I shake it off and limp toward my boss's office. Thankfully, there's light under the door and I can hear him talking.

I peek inside the cracked door and he looks up, phone cradled against his ear. When he holds up his index finger, I slip into his office and settle against the wall.

He's off the phone in about a minute. "Welcome back, Alexis. Did you have a nice time seeing your sister?"

"Um." I mean, technically I have seen my sister. But that's not what he's asking. Not what he's assuming. "I didn't go to San Francisco, Nate."

He frowns. "I thought—"

"I misled you. And I'm sorry." I push my fingers across my brow. My scalp itches from this stupid hat. "I went on that cruise with Dax."

At this, his eyebrows shoot to the North Pole. "Oh. I didn't realize …"

"It's a long story." I scratch behind my ear. "Do you know if … he's coming in today?"

The confusion stays bunched on his face, but he nods. "Should be. I think he was going to stop by Jenny's house this morning to make sure she was feeling okay first."

Jenny. As in, Dax's mom, who had a relapse while Dax was gone. She was so high on pills that she called up Lilith—who was in town to visit her family for Thanksgiving. Apparently, she thought they were still together. Lilith went over there to be with her, and since Jenny knew where Dax was, Lilith called Dax to let him know his mom needed him.

I was a fool, all right. But not because I trusted Dax.

Because I didn't.

I inhale a shaky breath. "Okay. Thanks." Turning, I pause, place my hand on the wall. "And I'm sorry about your sister, Nate."

He steeples his fingers, studies me. "It's been a long road to recovery for her, and I'm sad that she relapsed. She relies a lot on Dax—too much, if you ask me. That boy's been cleaning up her messes with much more compassion than I've ever been able to."

"Don't discount all the good you've done in his life, Nate. Like hiring him on here."

His lips quirk, and in that gesture, I see the family resemblance with Dax. "I was always under the distinct impression that you hated the fact I hired my nephew."

"Yeah, well." I shrug. "People change." And so do their perspectives, when they don't allow themselves to be blinded by their past.

I turn to head back to my office—and stop, my whole body going cold.

Dax is there, just about to go into his office next door to mine. I've gotten so used to seeing him in swim trunks, but he is still devastating in slacks and a button-down rolled to his elbows. His eyes roam all the way up to my beanie, back to my face. Then, without a word, he swoops into his office and shuts the door.

I deserve that and more.

But here's hoping that all of that rom-com watching of his will be in my favor.

Lifting a plea skyward, I square my shoulders and walk into his office. I've always hated the dove-gray color of his walls, always thought it was so very conformative of him, but now that I know him, I see it differently. It's calm and steady and dependable, just like him. And there are pops of red all around that I ignored before—a red stapler, red pen cup, red coffee mug.

Even his office was showing me all along that there is more to Dax Nyhart than I knew.

And I blew it. One hundred percent blew it.

He's already in his chair when I come inside. Forces out a breath. "What do you want, Alexis?"

No RB. No joking tone. No spark or sizzle in his eyes. Not even hurt swirling in the depths. The mask is back and I want to march up and rip it off with my bare hands.

But it's going to take more than Hurricane Alexis storming in and demanding things. This time, I'm the one in the wrong. And I have to make it right.

I lick my lips. "I talked to Janet and Cecilia last night."

Dax picks up a Rubik's cube from his desk, leans back in his chair. Doesn't say a word. Just looks at me, expression flat.

"First, I apologized to them for our lies." That was much harder than I thought. Even though both ladies already knew we weren't engaged because Dax had told Tom on Sunday night, they both sniffled a bit at our deception. Then they'd insisted that even though we weren't getting married, they saw how much he cared for me. When I said I wasn't so sure because of Lilith's call, they told me what had really happened. "They were really sweet and forgiving."

"Yeah, they're like that."

Nothing more. Just four words. Okay. "They also told me about your mom."

There. A flicker of emotion.

"How is she?"

It's a while before he answers. "Fine. Headed back to rehab after the holiday." His lips pull taut. "I tried to stay with her but she wouldn't let me. Said she's the mom and she's finally ready to take responsibility for herself." A sigh. "I think this one really affected her. Scared her."

"I'm so sorry."

He blinks, straightens, as if he's just realized we are talking like normal. Like he forgot he was mad at me. "Yeah, well. I'm just thankful Lilith was there. She stopped her from taking more pills and took her to the hospital."

The mention of Lilith is a blow. But he's right. Of course it's better that Lilith was there. "I'm glad she got the help she needed."

A sardonic laugh leaves his lips, curt and soft. "Okay, then. Good chat. I've got work now, so ..."

I hate this so much. But I can't avoid the rest of the conversation, can't just pretend that the cruise and those kisses and those conversations didn't happen. "Janet and Cecilia also told me Fred and Tom offered you the job regardless of the lies."

"They did." He coughs.

"That's kind of amazing. And surprising."

When Cecilia mentioned it, my jaw dropped. *"Why would they do that?"*

"Because after many years on this earth, they know that a

person owning up to their mistakes is just as important as not making them in the first place. Maybe even more important. And because they trust their instincts."

They also said they'd found a place for Landon and Gloria at the company, because after the cruise, we all were family to them.

Of course, the unspoken question … would *I* still be part of the family?

Oh, I hope so.

"So." I tap my fingers on his desktop. "Are you going to take it?"

"Yeah, but why do you care? Whether I take that one or the job in Texas, all of my accounts are yours." He sets down the cube and turns to his computer. "Speaking of that …"

Oh, Dax. I hurt him so badly, didn't I?

I swallow. "Before you do, I have a proposition for you."

He stills at my use of his own wording over a month ago when he first asked me to play pretend with him. How did I not recognize it then as the life-changing moment it was? The silence stretches and bends, and I am practically on my tiptoes with the tension until he finally speaks. "Not interested."

Well, great. I didn't expect that. In the scenario I imagined, his eyes would dance with humor, his full lips would turn into a grin, and we would joke and flirt and I could apologize and maybe, just maybe, he'd agree to my proposition.

But he doesn't want me. Doesn't want this. My

mistake was too great to be fixed with some unrealistic rom-com ending.

"Okay. Sorry to bother you." I hightail it back to my office, sit in my chair. Blink. What now? How do I tape back the pieces of my heart? Can't move forward, can't go back. I'm stuck. Just like Dad was stuck all those years.

"I know you, Alexis. You fight for what you want." Dax's accusation attacks my mind's eye. *"So is it really so easy for you to walk away like this?"*

I practically leap from the chair and barrel into his office again. He's still just sitting there, staring at his computer, but his head whips around when I slam the door behind me. "You're right. I do fight for what I want, Dax." I move across from him, lay my palms flat on the desk, and lean in, forcing him to look me in the eye—to know that I'm not going anywhere as long as there's a shred of hope that he will forgive me. "And I want you."

There's a tick in his jaw.

"Seeing how much you love rom-coms, I assumed you'd be rather partial to a good grand gesture. Unfortunately, I couldn't get a marching band and soccer field on such short notice, nor could I find a boombox to hold up outside your window—afraid the pawn shop was fresh outta those."

The golden flecks in his irises kindle.

"I'm not marrying your amnesic brother, so I can't declare my love for you in front of your whole family at our hospital wedding." I straighten and take a step sideways. Then another, until I've rounded the desk and stand in front of the chair he's occupying. "And I'm not a newspaper columnist who can invite you onto a baseball field for a kiss after pretending I was a student and —rather disturbingly, might I add—luring you into a relationship."

That one gets him. A small smile cracks his defenses.

But much as I've joked, this next part is going to take courage. "So I did this instead." I rip off my hat and my hair streams down in ribbons around me.

My very brown, very plain hair.

Kennedy and I made a late-night visit to the store and she helped me figure out what I couldn't even rightly remember.

His eyebrows contract together.

Guess this requires an explanation. *Here goes.* "You asked me once what my natural hair color is. Well, here it is. Poopy, unimpressive brown. This is me. This is it."

Dax is still just watching me, as if waiting for … more.

Okay. I take a strand of the hair, brush my fingertips against it. "It's the one thing I haven't told anyone else, except Kennedy who knew me before. And this doesn't mean I want to keep it this color, necessarily. But I want you to know, because even if you don't want me to be part of your life anymore, my hair color has been a stupid symbol to me of sorts, something keeping me from being the girl I once was. One who loved without reserve, without worry. And now it sounds really dumb coming from my mouth, but … what I'm saying is … I want you to know me, Dax." My lips tremble and oh great, I'm going to cry, aren't I? "And that's freaking scary, because it means I really care about you and you have so much potential to hurt me. And I have potential to hurt you, just like I've done. I'm so sorry I didn't believe you. I just … but my past is no excuse and—"

"RB." Dax stands in a flash, and before I can reconcile it, he's there in front of me, reaching for a lock of my hair, rubbing it between his fingers. "It's not 'poopy brown.' It's vibrant, with reds and blacks and so many colors threaded through it. Can't you see that you're more than even you know?"

"Dax," I whisper. "I'm so sorry."

Then he pulls me into his arms and I'm home. I let the tears fall, soaking his shirt, soaking him, but he doesn't seem to mind as his fingers first encircle my waist, then travel up and down my back in a soothing caress.

Gah, why did I resist this for so long?

After he kisses me, long and slow, he leans back against the desk and I stand in front of him. His thumbs make lazy circles on my hips. "So what's that proposition you were talking about?"

I laugh and push away evidence of my tears. My nose is stuffed and I'm sure my eyes are red, but this is also me. And it's refreshing to not hide it from him anymore. "Oh, nothing much." Tilting my head, I scratch my chin. "Just you and me. Forever." I wait a beat. "Or actually dating at least. Long distance. Short distance. Medium distance. I don't care. I just want to be where you are, Dax. I want to hold your hand and not worry that it's all for show. I want to snuggle and watch your terrible movies and my awesome ones together on the regular—yes, I know it's not the cool thing to say, but I'm saying it anyway. And"—I inch closer till I'm right up against him, my arms wrapped around his shoulders, our faces inches apart—"I want the freedom to kiss you whenever I darn please because you're my man and no one else's."

"I'll do it." His lips hover over mine. "But I have stipulations."

A delighted laugh bubbles in my chest. "I wouldn't expect any less. Let's hear them."

"One: We see each other every weekend if possible. You visit me. I visit you. And if every weekend isn't feasible, then every other is as long as I'm willing to go without being near you."

"Hmm." I play with the hair at the nape of his neck. "Okay. Next?"

"Two: We become those really annoying people who text hourly, talk daily, and kiss as much as possible, even in public."

With a shrug, I rub his earlobe between my finger and thumb. "I could maybe get behind that one."

"Three." I sense the change in his tone, from teasing to a bit more serious. "After a period of time to be mutually agreed upon, we consider our long-term options. You moving to LA, for instance."

Am I willing to do that? The idea of leaving my home, my friends, is probably the scariest thing ever. Then again, maybe starting over, finding a job that suits me better, might be a blessing in disguise, one I'd never seek out on my own. I don't know the answer, but he's not asking me to commit to that right now. He's only asking me to have a conversation about it. I give him a little nod, approval to continue.

He kisses my cheek. "Or I get a different job. Or we get the Bennetts to let me work remote. Or any number of options that put us together all the time. That lead to a real future together."

Whew. So he *does* see a future with me just like I do with him. I clear my now-dry throat. "Any others?"

"Just one more. Number four: We talk. If you're feeling a certain way, I'd so much rather you tell me than walk away."

Biting my lip, I nod. "I'm sorry again."

"Me too." Dax absently pushes my hair behind my shoulder, his thumb brushing along my collarbone, filling me with delicious warmth in all the right places. "Well? What do you think of my stipulations?"

"I'll have to take them under advisement." I scrunch my nose. "And by that I mean, I love them."

Dax pulls me closer. "I love *you*," he whispers.

I sigh against his lips. "I love you, too." Kiss him. Flash him my sweetest smile while batting my eyelashes. "Booger Bear."

"Aw, RB." He sets our foreheads together. "Winning a game of poker has never felt so good."

"Actually, I think *I'm* the winner." I press a kiss to one corner of his mouth, then the other.

"It's always a competition with you."

"And don't you forget it." I lean in. "Read 'em and weep, baby."

epilogue

. . .

Kennedy

I LOVE ALEXIS, and I am super happy for her right now. But if I have to watch her kiss Dax one more time today, I think I might scream. Is this how she felt being around Brooks and me the last two years?

Who am I kidding? Brooks never looked at me like Dax looks at her—like he's freaking privileged just to know her, much less be dating her.

When Dax—from the couch—asks if she got him a piece of pumpkin pie, Alexis rolls her eyes from the kitchen, where half of her friends (the non-pregnant ones) are dishing up Friends-giving Day dessert for their fiancés and half of them (the pregnant ones) are waiting in the living room for their husbands to bring them some. (Even Prince Topher and his sister Chloe are here with Lauren for a few days, as is Topher's body-guard, Frederick, who can't keep his eyes off the princess. Wonder what's going on there …)

Then there's me, inching closer to the front door with

my phone in my pocket and a plate of pie I got for myself. Nobody to be responsible for me. Nobody to be responsible for.

My eyes burn. Ugh, so annoying. I do not want to cry over that jerk Brooks ever again, but does my stupid body listen to me? Nooooo, it just goes on leaking tears for a guy who has already moved on from me, if his Instagram account can be believed.

Which is why I have to make this phone call. I can't trespass on my sister's goodwill and kindness too long.

I reach for the front door handle just as Alexis waltzes in with a plate and plops onto Dax's lap. He sets his chin on her shoulder. "For me?"

She forks a piece and holds it close to his lips. When he goes to bite it, she zooms it into her own mouth instead, groans. "Connor! This pie is amazing."

Dax says something low and throaty in her ear, and her eyes light up. "Dare," she says.

Oh, those two. They're impossibly adorable. I hope they get married and provide me with dozens of adorable nieces and nephews. But right now, it hurts my insides to see the five happy couples (maybe six if Freddy and Chloe are a secret thing?), so I open the door and duck outside into the nippy November afternoon. I've been here nearly two weeks and haven't really spent much time outside, but being from San Francisco means the cold doesn't bother me.

The porch is small but covered and a bit raised off the ground given that Alexis lives in a hilly neighborhood. Setting my pie down on the porch railing, I zip up my white Burberry jacket, a gift from my super-rich maternal grandma for my twenty-second birthday. (That was before I moved in with Brooks. For my twenty-third, she sent me a bridal catalog—a not-so-subtle hint that showed her traditional roots.) Then I slip into one of the two white wicker chairs with faded floral pads and pull the plate onto my lap. This is going to serve as delicious fortitude before I make the dreaded call.

I breathe in, let my shoulders settle. Finally. Peace and—

Nails clatter up the porch steps and all I see is a black face and a flash of white teeth before there's a huge dog leaping up at me. "Ah!" I scream, crossing my arms and lifting them in the air to shield myself. "I'll give you anything, just don't take my face."

"Finley!" There's a sharp whistle and the dog's head goes up. "Where are you, boy?"

"Over here!" I shift as I call, and my plate—and the pie along with it—falls to the wooden porch floor. The chocolate lab begins happily eating, its huge tail knocking into me.

"Excuse me, sir." I cross my arms over my chest. "That's my pie you're eating."

Someone groans to the left of me. "Finley."

My head jerks that way and I freeze. *Hello, Hottie McScottie.* The most delicious man I've ever seen is approaching the porch. And I live in a big city where there are lots of handsome men. But he's not attractive in the way that a lot of those city dwellers are—sculpted and waxed, with crisp suits and a dry martini in hand.

No, he's like that casual sort of effortlessly handsome, wearing simple, low-slung jeans that are nice and worn, and a red Oklahoma University hoodie. I can tell he's quite fit thanks to the strain of the cotton fabric. And his blond curls next to tan skin? Mmm, my personal Kryptonite. (In case you were wondering, no, Brooks isn't blond at all. A dark, brooding brow and pale skin, like a vampire without the sparkles.)

"I'm so sorry." The man sticks his hand through the porch railing and grabs the dog's collar. "Finley, that's not yours." His sentences are colored with a light Southern flare.

"At this point, you might as well let him finish it."

"He's normally so well behaved, but he's still a puppy. A big one, but only a year old and—" His eyes flit to me, back to the dog. Then zero in on me again. "You don't live here."

I raise an eyebrow, push my hair behind an ear. "My sister owns the house and I'm staying … a while." Right now, Alexis and I are sharing her room, her bed. It's been nice to have a place to retreat to, and I haven't really decided what I'm doing. I figure if she's okay with it, maybe I'll stay through the holidays at the very least.

Of course, I need money to do even that. I love influencing, but it doesn't pay all the bills, especially in California. A flash of heat sears through me at the thought that I spent so much money—all of my inheritance from my dad—on my life with Brooks. And with him spreading nasty rumors about me, my online credibility has started taking a hit. I've somehow got to turn this around. Alexis may think she should be taking care of me, but I've been taking care of myself my whole life. I'm not going to mooch off of her.

But that's a problem for another moment. Not this one. "I'm Kennedy."

"Oh." The man's light blue eyes keep holding onto me. I notice crinkles around the corners, like maybe he smiles a lot. I'd clock his age about early to mid-thirties—so, like Alexis and her friends, about a decade older than me. "I'm Ryan. The neighbor." With his free hand, he points to the house to our left.

"Ah! The hot doctor neighbor who runs around without his shirt on? I've heard a lot about you."

A deep flush spreads all the way up to his cheeks. "I don't know about that." He rubs a hand over his neck, and I get the distinct feeling he's uncomfortable. Fascinating. But what does he expect with a house full of women and a body like the one I suspect is lurking under his clothing? "I mean, yeah. I'm a doctor. And a neighbor. And I do run a lot. But …"

"The hot part?"

"Yeah. I don't know about that."

"Well, I'm a very objective third party, and I can confirm the truth of that statement. And I haven't even seen you without a shirt on."

He coughs. "Um."

I kind of want to giggle at his old-man modesty. Most guys who look like him would be strutting all around the yard crowing like a rooster about now. Leaning down, I pick up the plate that's been licked clean of crumbs thanks to young Finley here. Now that Ryan's mentioned it, the dog's paws do look slightly too big for his body in that goofy teenage way both dogs and kids have.

"Do you want to join us for Friends-giving?" I ask.

"What now?"

"My sister and her friends. They do it every year." We spent yesterday—actual Thanksgiving—with Dax's family. His mom and uncle are really nice, and it was awesome to see how well Alexis and Jenny got along. "Everyone brought over their leftovers to share. Come on. There's plenty."

"Oh, thank you, but I've got company coming over." A small black car pulls up to his driveway. "Yeah. I should head back." He lets go of Finley's collar, and the dog sits upright as a young girl and a beautiful, model-thin blonde woman climb from the car. With a bark, Finley bolts from the porch and the little girl squeals, dropping to her knees only to be tackled by the dog. Clearly they are well acquainted.

"Anyway. Sorry about the pie." Ryan scratches the back of his head. "And thanks for the invite. Tell everyone I say happy holidays."

"No problem. I will."

"Ryan!" The woman calls, waving—probably wondering who in the world he's talking to.

"Be right there." He turns to me, catches my gaze again. "Nice meeting you, Kennedy. Maybe I'll see you around."

Oh, goodness, I hope so. Nothing like a hot doctor to take one's mind off of no-good exes. "Mmm hmm," I say brilliantly.

He smiles and something shifts inside of me. Then

he turns and heads toward the people waiting, including the woman whose head is tilted in my direction. Upon closer inspection, she looks a bit haggard and ducks back into the car to say something. After a bit, a teenage girl with Air Pods and a cell phone gets out.

Can't be a wife and kids, with the way he called them "company." Maybe a girlfriend? Ryan gives them all hugs and, arm around the woman's shoulders, guides the group inside.

Le sigh. Why are all the hot decent men taken?

A breeze kicks up, rustling some dead leaves that have fallen from a tree in Alexis's front yard. I've stalled long enough. Pulling my phone from my coat pocket, I start to dial.

When she answers, I push on a smile because even though we're not video chatting, she'll know if I'm frowning. Says she can hear it in people's voices. And she's an amazing businesswoman who's had huge success, so I don't doubt it.

"Well, finally deigning to call me, are we?"

Ugh. "Hi, Gran. Happy Thanksgiving."

"A day late."

"Right. Yeah. Sorry about that." I add a little fake cheerleader pep to my voice and remember that she is always a fan of getting straight to the point. "So, I'd like to talk to you about my trust fund."

Hey, friend! Thanks so much for reading Alexis's and Dax's story. Reviews make all the difference, so if you enjoyed it, would you consider leaving one?

It's been so much fun writing about this group of friends in the California Dreamin' series, and I wasn't quite ready to let them go. Check out Kennedy's story in *Needing the Next-Door Neighbor*.

Want more of Alexis and Dax's happily ever after? Check out the bonus epilogue at kristincanary.com/officeenemy.

sneak peek

Needing the Next-Door Neighbor

So this is my life—serving lattes to teens who think they're better than me because they've got Daddy's credit card and the latest Dolce & Gabbana purse.

"I'm sorry, you want a what?" I tuck a piece of hair behind my ear and lean in. It's possible with the whirring of the grinder behind me and the chatter from patrons at other tables that I misheard the girl, who can't be more than twelve despite her midriff-baring purple shirt and tight jeans.

Not that I can judge. I also grew up way too fast.

The girl turns to her carbon copy friend and they both roll their eyes before she redirects her attention to me. "I said, I want a 20/20."

Okay, I might be fairly new to barista-ing at Java Awakening—an adorable San Diego coffee shop my sister Alexis and her friends frequent—but I still consider myself in the know about all things coffee.

"Oh, that must be new!" I snatch up a to-go cup and a Sharpie. "What's in it?"

"OMG, can you believe this lady?" the girl stage whispers to her friend.

Then, like I'm super old and hard of hearing, she says—nice and slow AND loud—"It's a latte with twenty pumps of vanilla and twenty pumps of hazelnut, whole milk, whip, and caramel drizzle." She smacks her gum and twirls her sleek black hair that's quite obviously been professionally cut and colored.

Must be nice. Over the last few months, the highlights in my brown hair have grown out, and its split ends hang past the spot just below my shoulders where I prefer it. But that's what happens when you're suddenly poor.

"Hey lady, you listening?"

I jump at her snappy attitude—and fingers. Oh my sheesh, I really, really want to say something sarcastic back to her. My manager Josh's wife Kayla probably would. I've seen her take people down a notch or two a few times. But I can't afford to lose the one source of income I have at the moment. Not that Josh would fire me. I don't think.

"Of course." Showing her the writing on the cup, I quirk an eyebrow.

"Fine. But make sure it's 190 degrees exactly or I'm asking for a refund." Little Miss Attitude glances down at her phone and starts furiously typing as if it isn't the rudest thing in the world.

But maybe nobody's ever taught her as much. Maybe she's just copying what she knows. A product of her environment. This mean girl, who is probably at the top of the food chain at her school, is most likely this way because she's trying to prove something. Or she's scared. Or unsure of who she is.

Or all of the above.

I know because I've been that girl. Not *mean*, per se, but putting on an act for the world to see. And for a long time, it served me well. Once upon a time, not so very long ago, I was the one with a closet full of new and expensive clothes, for whom restaurants and hotels comped meals and stays, just for a mere mention in my social media posts.

I had it all—until I didn't.

Now I'm here, aged twenty-three, sharing a small bedroom with my sister, working and saving to go back to college—which, at this point, won't happen for several years unless I can miraculously find another job that pays more than minimum wage. Alexis has offered to pay my way, but she's already done too much for me. So, unless Gran decides to release my trust fund, I'm doing this on my own.

Which is good. Because I've got to show everyone— myself included—that I can.

Way to be a bummer, Kennedy. Shrugging away my too-dreary thoughts, I flourish Little Miss Attitude's order onto a cup with the marker. "That'll be six-fifty-nine."

She hands me her daddy's credit card, and when I flash her a determined smile, you'd think I threatened her dog. Her narrowed eyes are proof that apparently she isn't used to people being nice in response to her sourness.

After her friend orders a 20/20 as well, they move aside, and I head for the espresso machine, where Josh Gregory is currently finishing up an order of his own. I respect that he's the kind of manager who gets his hands dirty and doesn't just boss us all around from on high. When I come into his periphery, he flashes me a tired smile. "How's it going, Kennedy?"

"Just another Wednesday in paradise."

He chuckles, but ironically, I think he believes this *is* paradise. His uncle owns the coffee shop from afar, and Josh loves nurturing the space. While many guys would want to climb corporate ladders, he's content with his life. And why shouldn't he be? He's got a brand-new baby girl and an intelligent, smoking-hot wife who quite literally can't keep her hands off of him.

"Well, thanks again for covering extra hours so I could take some paternity leave." Josh pushes his thick glasses farther up on his nose and lets loose a yawn. "Kayla and I appreciated knowing you and the others had things under control those few weeks I was out." He collects his three drinks and handles them like a pro, not spilling a drop. But then he just stands there, blinking, like he forgot what he's supposed to do with them.

"No problem at all. Just let me know if you still need some extra coverage." I cock my head, smile. "Seems you could use the rest."

And I could use the money. Being a barista is actually kind of fun—it reminds me a little bit of waitressing at the high-end bar where I worked briefly before meeting Brooks in San Francisco a few years ago—but it pays absolute beans (no pun intended), especially when I can only get twenty hours in a normal week.

If I ever hope to rebuild my life, to save enough to resume college, to eventually get a degree that qualifies me for a job that pays actual money to live on, I definitely need to get another job now—either a full-time one or something else that's part-time, like the retail job I worked over the holidays.

Of course, I could always take the position Gran offered me two months ago. But I have my reasons for saying no. Not reasons that Marsha Montgomery understands. But reasons that are all mine.

"Thanks." Josh nods as he balances the drinks in his hands against his long-sleeved *Star Wars* T-shirt. "I'll keep your offer in mind. Rey still hasn't gotten her days and nights straight."

"I've heard that's pretty common." In fact, Evie Bryant—who, along with Kayla, used to live in Alexis's house before she got married—said the same thing. She had little baby Fitz on January fifth, just ten days before Kayla gave birth to Rey. (And yes, they both named their babies after fictional characters: Fitzwilliam Darcy from *Pride & Prejudice* and Rey from the newest round of *Star Wars* films.)

While Josh serves his drinks to the waiting customers, I crank out the two "20/20s" and then deliver them with all the chipper spunk I can manage. My life may be lame, but I've dealt with a lot worse things than snarky teen girls in my twenty-three years, and it costs me nothing to be nice to them. Who knows?

Maybe it'll remind them they are more than the things they pretend to be. Maybe I can perform a little tiny miracle and brighten their day.

Little Miss Attitude snatches her drink, takes a sip. Frowns. Wrinkles her nose. "Ugh."

Her friend does the same. "Double ugh."

They both tighten their grip on their purse straps, flip their hair over their shoulders, and flounce from the coffee shop into the cloudy California afternoon.

Welp. A miracle maker, I am not.

With a sigh, I move back to the register and take the next order. For the next few hours, there's a steady stream of customers, including Kayla and Rey, who surprise Josh with a visit. Despite having just had a baby a few weeks ago, the woman is gorgeous with her long torso and brown hair that's pulled back in a pony-tail—albeit with something white and crusty that is quite possibly dried spit-up or old milk in her bangs.

She comes behind the counter and steps up to give Josh a kiss, and I don't miss how her hand darts around to his backside and squeezes his butt. He kisses her back, then leans down to nuzzle the sleeping baby in the stroller before attending to the lone customer in line at the moment.

"And there's Kennedy, our lifesaver!" Kayla turns to me and leans in for a quick hug. I don't know why this still takes me by surprise. Even though she's Alexis's friend, not mine, all of them—Kayla, Evie, Shelby, Lauren, and Alexis—have welcomed my extended stay here with open arms. Still, I never want to make assumptions about where I stand.

Where I belong.

I mean, I know Alexis and I are bonded forever, even if she's just my half-sister. Our dad died in a plane accident when I was just four years old. That's when Alexis discovered her father had another family—my mom Pippa and me. But instead of turning away from me, hating me, she claimed me. Loved me in spite of it all.

And I'll never be able to repay her for that.

Now that Mom's been gone for five years, the only people I really have are Alexis and Gran. One loves me unconditionally. The other ... well, let's just say she's undecided about me at the moment.

Who am I kidding? She's been undecided about me from the moment I was born. To her, I'm just Pippa 2.0.

A disgrace to the Montgomery name.

I pull back from Kayla and glance down at Rey, whose dark curls match Josh's and whose perfect little nose is a replica of Kayla's. She is absolute perfection, not because of her looks, but because she was the product of true love. A love that gives and sacrifices and constantly chooses each other.

Someday, I hope Rey knows how lucky she is.

I touch her soft cheek. "She's amazing."

"She is—even when she bites my boobs and makes sure I don't sleep a wink."

Looking up, I expect Kayla to wear a joking expression. But she's completely serious.

"That sounds ... kind of awful."

She sighs. "And equally wonderful. Such is motherhood."

"Hmm." My fingers find the small gold cross necklace at my throat—the one my mom gave me for my eighteenth birthday just before she died from a quick bout with cancer. "Well, it's good to see you out and about."

"I was absolutely dying being shut away in that house alone—well, you know what I mean. Without adult interaction." Kayla squeezes my elbow. "Josh told me we could go out to dinner after closing."

I check my watch. "That's not that far off. I can cover the rest of the shift alone if you want to take off now."

"Really?" Kayla throws her arms around me again—in an almost desperate way—and I catch a faint whiff of baby powder and soap. "You're the best. Although actually, if you'd like to join us, you are more than welcome. I have a text out to the gang to see if anyone else can meet up. I think Shelby and Eric have a late meeting or something at the school, but Evie's ready to rejoin the land of the living again too. Want to come?"

"Oh, that's really nice." But how do I say that I just can't deal with the noise tonight? And what's wrong with me? I used to live for the party scene, the social interactions. Lately though, the perfect evening consists of a glass of wine and binging old episodes of *The Bachelor*. "I think Chloe and I were going to hang out at the house, though."

Hopefully Chloe won't mind me using her as an excuse. The current princess—yeah, you heard me ... a real live princess—of Kentonia and her bodyguard Tia are crashing at Alexis's house so she can spend time with her future sister-in-law Lauren and "escape her royal duties for a while." She's the other "outsider" in the group, though you wouldn't know it with her vivacious personality and flawless style. But it's been nice to not feel like the only one in "the gang" who isn't an original housemate.

Frowning, Kayla pulls her phone from the diaper bag hanging from the stroller handle. "I thought Chloe was coming to dinner with us."

"Really? That's odd." If that's true, then I actually might have the house to myself tonight—a rarity. "I'll text her and see what's up." I should probably just be honest with Kayla. Hopefully it doesn't make her think less of me. "I'm pretty zonked today too. Think I need some quiet time at home."

She studies me for a while. "You doing okay?"

My fingers itch at the scrutiny and I move toward the sink to wash up some dishes. "Asks the woman who just gave birth." Grabbing a huge smoothie pitcher, I dunk it into the soap suds.

"I can still tell when someone else is having a rough day. You thinking about your no-good ex?"

"Yes. And no. It's just"—I use a long-handled scrubber to nudge out a stuck piece of frozen fruit from beneath the blender's blade at the bottom—"everything."

"Still trying to figure out where you belong?"

Dang. Is this woman a mind reader? "Something like that." Because not only do I need to figure out my future—where I want to live, what I want to do, where I want to go to school, who I want to be—but I need to do it all in such a way that the family I have left is proud of me. Alexis has provided a safe space for the last few months, but she and Dax are getting more serious. She's gone half the time to visit him in Los Angeles.

She knows me better than anyone else, but I'm the only one who can create a real future for myself.

No pressure, right?

I scrub harder and, once the fruit piece comes free, rinse it and the soap down the empty side of the sink.

"Let me tell you something I had to learn the hard way, okay, Ken?" Kayla uses my nickname effortlessly, like she actually knows me—not just the me I project out to the world, but the real me. Then again, she's a dating coach for a living, so she's probably used to dealing with hot messes like me. "You belong with the people who love you for who you are—and they won't leave. So rely on them." She pauses. "On us."

Okay, well, that was unexpected. And beautiful. I set the clean but wet blender upside down on the drying rack. Glance over at her. "Thanks, Kayla."

"You got it, girlfriend." A tiny, fussing coo rises from the stroller. In seconds, it becomes a wail. "And that's my cue to feed my baby." She grabs the stroller handles and begins to maneuver it toward the kitchen, likely headed to Josh's office in the back. "Feel free to come to dinner when you get off if you change your mind. I'll text you the location once we decide where we're going."

"I will. Thanks."

She disappears, and a half hour later, the little family of three is out the main door. I serve a handful of new customers, clean up the machines, and politely usher out a few stragglers. After I lock up, I hustle against the cold air for my car—a beat-up yellow Toyota that once belonged to my mom. When I climb inside, I start it up and relish the heat pumping from the vents. San Diego's temps might be temperate, but the evenings can still get chilly with the wind coming off the Pacific.

My phone buzzes in my purse. I reach for it and groan when I see a text from Gran—a picture of a gorgeous office overlooking the San Francisco bay. And a note: *A life of respectability awaits you once you've decided to dry your eyes and act like a Montgomery.*

Just like I do with all of her texts lately—one or two a week with messages that are just as passive-aggressive —I ignore this one and lock my phone. Then I turn on the radio and blare 'N Sync, an old-school boy band that Lauren and Chloe tell me I've just gotta try.

I somewhat see the appeal as I race down the freeway to *Pop*.

Sure, I might be single and broke and sharing a queen-sized bed with my older sister who thinks she has to take care of me, but at least here, I'm free. Brooks wasn't what I would call abusive, but he also didn't give me space to be me.

And I didn't demand it, either. I was too afraid to lose him.

Then I did.

But I don't regret it. I don't miss him. Being here has given me the time and perspective I need to see what an unhealthy relationship it was.

I head toward Point Loma and before I know it, I'm back at Alexis's house. Nobody else's car is in the driveway—so I really *do* have the rare night at home alone.

It sounds completely glorious. Does that make me totally lame?

Hauling myself and my stuff out of the car, I head to the darkened front porch. Canned laughter drifts from the windows of the house next door—the house where the hottest doctor known to man lives. Dr. Ryan Rosche, who I've only spoken to once a few months ago but have waved casually to now and again when we're both coming and going … or when he's in his backyard throwing a ball to his black Labrador Finley … or when he's leaving for a shirtless run around the neighborhood and I happen to drive past … slowly.

Still, more than just being handsome, his best feature is his kind smile. Of course, he doesn't only use it on me. He also uses it on the woman I assume is his girlfriend and her daughters. I've also seen them coming and going quite frequently.

Which means that the guy is clearly off-limits. Because I'm not a man stealer. Not like Mom. Alexis claims that Pippa didn't know my dad was married with a kid when she got with him, but I honestly have my doubts.

Still, whenever I *do* get back into the dating game, I want it to be with a guy like Ryan—genuine, friendly, and caring. Someone whose smile makes the world a better place. Who cares about more than his number of social media followers and his bank account.

So, basically, the opposite of Brooks Marsden.

"Okay, Kennedy, stop being weird and go inside."

Yes, I talk to myself sometimes, all right? Thankfully nobody is here to witness my insanity.

I shove open the front door—and nearly scream at the sight of someone sitting on our couch.

Guess I'm not alone after all.

books by kristin canary

California Dreamin' Series

Enamoring Her Amnesic Ex (prequel)

Loving the Ladies' Man

Desiring His Dating Coach

Saving the Secret Prince

Belonging With Her Best Friend

Engaging the Office Enemy

Needing the Next-Door Neighbor

Hallmark Beach Series

Beachside Kisses With My Bodyguard

about the author

Kristin is a wife and boy mom who functions best on peach tea and cookie dough ice cream. A desert dweller, she always has her eye on the next trip to a beach somewhere—and if she can't travel there in person, then you'd better believe she's going to write about it. Kristin is never fully satisfied with a movie, TV show, or book without a hefty dose of romance in it, and she's grateful to be living a true-life love story with her own crazy little family. Connect with her at KristinCanary.com.

facebook.com/kristincanary
instagram.com/kristincanaryauthor